Books by Willo Davis Roberts

The Magic Book

Willo Davis Roberts

THE MAGIC BOOK

1986 ATHENEUM *New York*

Library of Congress Cataloging-in-Publication Data

Roberts, Willo Davis.   The magic book.

SUMMARY: When Alex and his friends try the spells
in an old book, things don't happen quite as
they'd thought, but they decide to try
the bully spell on the school bully anyway.
[1. Magic—Fiction. 2. Bullies—Fiction] I. Title.
PZ7.R54465Mag 1986   [Fic]   85-20056
ISBN 0-689-31120-6

Published simultaneously in Canada by
Collier Macmillan Canada, Inc.
Composition by Yankee Typesetters, Concord, New Hampshire
Printed and bound by
Fairfield Graphics, Fairfield, Pennsylvania
Designed by Mary Ahern
First Edition

The Magic Book

1

I F I had known ahead of time what I'd be getting into, I'm not sure I would have gone with my dad to that used book sale.

It was the Saturday before school started, and Dad had offered to take me fishing. I agreed right away, and then he said, "We'll go just as soon as I check out the used book sale at the library."

I groaned. "If we go there first, we'll never get to the lake."

"Oh, sure we will. The sale starts at nine. We can be out of there within an hour, Alex."

"Why don't we go fishing first? Get up early, and . . ."

"Saturday's my day off. I don't want to get up early. And I want to look over the used books. I always get some bargains," Dad said.

When I looked to my mom for help, she only shrugged. So we went to the book sale.

I didn't expect the day to be a success. Dad gave me

a couple of dollars when we went in the door and said, "Maybe you'll find something you want, Alex. I'll meet you back at the main door in an hour, OK?"

I knew he wouldn't meet me in an hour unless I went looking for him. Turn him loose in a book store or library and he may not come out until you send in a St. Bernard to rescue him. They had the sale in the auditorium in the basement, with the books laid out on long tables, and Dad disappeared almost as soon as we went in.

There were lots of people there already, trying to get the best books before someone else saw them. My friend Jeff was with his grandmother; he saw me and waved but didn't come over. He was going to have his twelfth birthday in a few days; I figured he was buttering up his grandma so she'd give him what he wanted for his birthday, the way she usually did.

I was stuck for at least an hour. I wandered around, looking at old math books, a history book on the Revolutionary War that looked old enough to have been written while it was going on, cookbooks for stuff like the rich desserts my mom never makes and two hundred ways to cook with zucchini. I picked up one book that was about interior decorating. I thought it might make a present for my mom; nobody in our family objects to a book being used as long as it has all the pages. This one was written in 1932, though, and it didn't look like anything Mom would ever use, so I put it back.

As I turned away from that table, a book slid off and landed at my feet. I don't know why, I swear I didn't touch it, but there it was on the floor. Several people turned to look at me, so I thought I'd better pick it up.

It was old, dark blue or faded black; it was impossible to say. It had once had gold lettering, but a lot of that had flaked off and I couldn't tell what it said. I stuck the book back on the table and turned toward the next display, which had some outdated science fiction on it. Maybe I'd find something there to spend my money on.

Behind me, there was a thud. Again, heads turned in my direction. I swung around and saw the old book on the floor once more.

What the heck? I spoke to the lady browsing through some music books a few yards away. "I didn't touch it," I said. She sort of pursed her mouth, and I knew she didn't believe me.

I picked up the book once more. This time I put it down firmly, well away from the edge of the table. It couldn't possibly fall off again.

It hit the floor before I finished the thought. It just slid right across that table and over the edge.

I stared at it, aware that some of the book shoppers were giving me very disapproving looks now. One lady even said, "He looks old enough to know how to behave in a library."

My face was hot as I knelt to reach for the book. I wasn't going to pick it up again, I was going to shove it under the table and forget about it.

Only this time the book had fallen with the front cover standing open, and something was written on the inside that I read without even intending to.

In a spidery hand on a yellowing page, I read "This book belongs to Alexander W. Graden."

The prickling started at the base of my spine and worked upward; by the time it reached my head, my hair was standing up on end.

My middle name is William, and we're the only Graden family in town.

I was still kneeling there, frozen like the insects my little brother Mike freezes in ice cubes until he's ready to sketch them. I'm not sure I even remembered to breathe.

It gave me a very peculiar feeling to see my name written out in this old, old book as if it had been put there a hundred years ago.

"Alex? What the heck are you doing?"

I glanced up to see Jeff standing beside me. "Look at this," I said, sounding strangled.

Jeff dropped down beside me and read what my unsteady finger pointed out. "How come your book is being sold? Did you donate it to the library?"

"It's not my book, you idiot. Look at it. Published in London in 1802, more than a hundred and seventy years before I was born. I never saw it before."

"Then how'd it get your name in it?"

"How do I know? Jeff, it kept falling off the table, and I'm positive I never touched the thing."

"Are there more Alexander W. Gradens? Maybe it belonged to your grandfather."

"My grandfather's name was Samuel, and he lived in Minnesota. Besides, how would a book of his get to Washington State even if the name was right? I don't have any ancestors with the same name as mine. I was named for a friend of my dad's. Jeff, you pick it up and put it back on the table."

He stared at me. Usually Jeff is game for anything. I haven't very often seen him chicken out at one of my suggestions. We've been friends all our lives, and when we were about nine his mother referred to us as the Terrible Twosome. This time he didn't make any move to touch the book.

He swallowed audibly. "Alex, did you notice the name of this thing?"

I hadn't, but now I did. There in funny looking letters above the spidery writing was the title: MAGIC SPELLS AND POTIONS FOR THE BEGINNER.

My voice sounded hollow as I tried to laugh. "Well, if it comes to magic, I guess I'm a beginner, all right."

Suddenly, without either of us touching it—and we didn't blow on it, either—a few pages flipped over. Only they did it slowly, as if a ghostly hand had reached out with invisible fingers—

I inhaled sharply and sat back on my heels. Jeff, however, leaned forward and squinted to read the fine print.

"*Spell to put an end to a bully's ways,*" he read, then poked me with an elbow. "Hey, Alex, you better buy this and take it home. Maybe it'll tell you how to get rid of Norm Winthrop."

I got a cramp in my stomach just thinking about Norm. He'd made my life miserable all last year, and it had been a big relief when school was out and I didn't have to see him every day. I rubbed my left elbow, the one he'd hit with the lunch room door, and then told the supervisor it was an accident, though there was a window in the door and he'd been able to see me, all right. I could still feel how much it had hurt, and remember how hard it had been to pretend it didn't.

I didn't want the book. It gave me the creeps just to be kneeling there on the floor with it. But I found myself closing it and picking it up and walking toward the table where they took your money.

For fifty cents I bought the book that was going to change my whole life in ways I never suspected.

WE didn't catch any fish on Saturday. I knew we wouldn't, when we had to take our books home first and didn't even get to the lake until nearly eleven o'clock. My dad didn't especially care; he likes to sit in the sun in a small boat and do nothing, where nobody can reach him to ask him to mow the lawn or fix the washing machine or make a decision about anything. He says that's what he does all week, make decisions and see about fixing things at the trucking firm where he's a partner with my grandfather, and Saturdays are his days off.

When we got home, my sister Dorothy—pardon me, Deidra, she gave herself that name a year ago when she got to be fourteen—gave him a message. There was a truck broken down in Bellingham, and did he want the driver to call a mechanic or what?

Dad muttered under his breath about drivers who had to be baby-sat and went on through the house to the kitchen phone. I stuck my head in the refrigerator and started hauling out stuff for a snack.

"It's only an hour until dinner," my sister said. "We're having spaghetti."

"I'll be hungry again by then," I promised and piled up cheese and baloney and lettuce on a slice of cracked wheat bread.

I carried my sandwich upstairs and found my little brother in the room we shared, building a model airplane.

I flopped on my bed, thinking I'd look through that stupid book I'd brought home, only it wasn't there on my nightstand where I'd put it.

"What'd you do with my book?" I demanded.

Mike's eyes were magnified by his glasses; he didn't even look up. "I don't know what you're talking about."

"That big, thick old dark-blue book that was right here."

"I didn't do anything with any book," Mike said. He was using tweezers to place a tiny part on the model. I resisted the urge to throw a pillow at him and make him pay attention to me.

"It's gone, and there hasn't been anybody here but you, has there? Think a minute, Mike. You must've done something with it."

I looked around the room, and there it was. Practically at his elbow on his desk. I grunted in disgust and reached for it, but he yelped just before I touched it.

"Don't move that! I'm using it to weight down those wing parts until the glue sets! Just give it a few more minutes, Alex."

He was always gluing something—often to my clothes or my homework papers—so I was used to the request.

"Don't you pay any attention to what you pick up for a weight?" I asked, knowing perfectly well he didn't.

"It'll only be a few minutes more," Mike said soothingly. "Read something else for a little while, Alex."

"I want to read that book," I told him. I didn't really want him to have to redo the plane wings, though, so I went back downstairs and called my friend Bucky Dollman. Bucky's real name is Sherman, which he hates, and for a while in third grade the kids called him "Doll," which he hated even worse, so he finally convinced a few key guys that he was going to answer only to Bucky. It took a few bloody noses—his as well as other people's—to enforce it, but he's been Bucky to everybody but the teachers for a long time now.

"Come on over," Bucky said. "I've got a new video game."

So I went over, and we played for an hour, and I was late for supper. My appetite was good, though, even if the spaghetti was sort of lukewarm.

There was a movie on TV Mike and I wanted to see; I didn't get back upstairs until about nine-thirty. The big faded old book wasn't on Mike's desk anymore, and I scowled at him.

"What did you do with it now?"

"Nothing. I left it right there," Mike insisted.

"Was Deidra in here?"

"How should I know? I was downstairs, watching the movie."

Still scowling, I walked across the hallway to my sister's room. She was on the phone, talking to her best friend Shirley, looking the way she usually did before she went to sleep. She was in yellow pajamas with her hair in pink rollers, and with the hand that wasn't holding the phone she was painting her toenails.

"Did you take a book out of my room?" I asked.

Deidra paused to look at me as if I were a snake that had crawled out of the closet. "I'm on the phone, Alex."

"And you'll be on it for an hour. I can't wait that long. Where's my book?"

"You mean that dusty old thing that was on Mike's desk?"

"Yeah, that one. Where is it?"

She sighed in an exaggerated way for Shirley's benefit. "Just a minute, Shirl. It didn't look like anything anybody'd miss, Alex. I borrowed it. Just until Monday, until Daddy can get a new leg for my bed. I needed something just that thick to hold up the corner when the leg broke."

I stared at her. "For crying out loud, it's a *book*. I got it to *read*. Did it ever occur to you to *ask* before you take things that belong to someone else?"

"It didn't look that important, and you were busy watching TV. As soon as I get a new leg, I'll give it back. Honest, Alex, I couldn't find anything else the right height, and I had to use it."

I gave up. I took a shower and went to bed, after I moved the jar off my pillow that had a gigantic brown spider in it. I was used to such things. Mike captured insects and animals all the time, to use as models for his sketching—he was pretty good for only nine-and-a-half—and he wasn't fussy about where he put the jars or the boxes down. I never came in and went to bed without turning on a light, just in case, not after the time I knocked over a jar of ants and the lid came off it.

I woke up an hour or so later when there was a loud thump and a muffled howl from across the hall.

Mom called up the stairs. "What was that?"

I got up and turned on the hall light, peering into my sister's bedroom.

Deidra was sitting up, sort of sliding out of bed, because it was tilted toward me. The old blue book that had been holding up the corner of it had slid across the floor almost to the doorway. I bent down and picked it up, though it sent a shiver through me to touch it, for some reason.

"Alex!" my sister yelled, but I wasn't going to give the book back to her.

"Deidra's bed fell down again," I called to Mom, and turned and walked back to my own room, putting the book on the nightstand where I'd left it before. I hadn't any more than let go of it when it slid off onto the floor.

I stared at it, my breath coming faster. "Don't start that here," I said.

"I didn't do anything," Mike muttered drowsily.

"Not you. The book," I said, but he was already asleep again.

I didn't want to pick up that book. I'd been crazy to waste fifty cents on it. Only a miracle would stop Norm Winthrop from picking on me, and I was pretty sure a dusty old book wasn't going to make a miracle.

Well, if it refused to stay on the table, it could stay on the floor, I thought. I kicked it, and then gasped, sinking onto the side of the bed and squeezing my toes to stop the pain. That fool book hadn't moved at all when I kicked it. It felt as if it were nailed right where it was.

I glared at it, wishing I'd put it back under my sister's bed. I let go of my toes and crawled under the blanket, pretending the book wasn't even there.

It was, though, and I couldn't forget it. It would really be something if it could actually give me a spell that worked. I remembered the time I'd spent all weekend writing out a history report, and on Monday Norm had knocked my folder out of my hands into a mud puddle and then stepped on it to make sure it got good and wet. Mrs. Critelli had said she was sorry, she couldn't read it that way, and I'd had to rewrite it. That hadn't been as bad as the time I'd left a folder full of homework on the edge of the sink in the restroom, though. I thought I was alone in there, or I wouldn't have done it. When I smelled the smoke, it was too late. Norm had knocked the folder into the wastebasket and then dropped a lighted match in on top.

Norm hadn't stuck around, naturally, and I couldn't prove he'd done it. Mr. Hamilton said lots of kids had dirty running shoes; the ones I'd seen might not have belonged to Norm, though I knew they had.

I'd never hated anybody before, not really, but I hated Norm.

I leaned over the edge of my bed, speaking in the darkness toward where I knew that book lay on the floor. "All right," I said to it. "Tomorrow I'll read you, and you better be good."

There was a soft chuckling sound. It couldn't have come from the book. It must have been Mike, dreaming.

I had a funny feeling, though, before I went back to sleep. I didn't know if I wanted to read the fool book or not. Wild as it seemed, I wondered if it might not be dangerous.

3

SUNDAY afternoon Uncle Charlie and Aunt Nola came over for a barbecue. I like barbecues—though my dad doesn't cook much in the kitchen, he's great in the backyard—but my cousins are a pain in the neck.

Freddie's four and Jerry's eight, and nothing is safe when they're around. If we'd had keys to our rooms, we'd have locked the doors until they were gone.

Since there were no keys, Mike put all his models as high up as he could find a place for them, and we hid stuff in the closet and hoped they wouldn't open that door. Deidra had junk all over her room that she didn't want them to touch, and no place to hide it, so she lectured Freddie and Jerry severely the minute they set foot in the house, telling them to stay out of her room.

Unfortunately, Mom heard her and gave her a lecture on hospitality. She said it wasn't very nice to talk to them that way before they'd even done anything, and Deidra said she remembered what they'd done last time when they got into her makeup and pretended they were clowns. And then Aunt Nola walked in, and they stopped talking. Deidra rolled her eyes at me. She knew what we were in for from Freddie and Jerry.

Mike and I had already decided we'd try to take turns guarding the stairs so they couldn't get to our room. Deidra just stayed in hers, talking on the telephone to Shirley.

Deidra has her own phone. My folks argued about that before she got it, because Dad didn't think a fifteen-year-old girl needed her own phone, and Mom said "But you make such a fuss if she's on *ours* more than a few minutes," and *he* said, "That's because I get emergency calls when a truck breaks down or something," and Mom said, "Then let her have her own, as long as she pays for it herself."

Deidra worked afternoons and Saturdays at the Burger Master. I decided when I got a regular job I was going to do something better with the money than pay for a telephone to talk to somebody as giggly as Shirley.

Mike was supposed to be watching the stairs when Freddie and Jerry decided they needed to use the upstairs bathroom. They said someone was in the downstairs one, so Mike let them go up.

"I told them to come straight back down, not to go in any other room," he assured me. That was right before we heard the loud *thump*, and a cry of pain.

"That didn't come from the bathroom," I said, brushing past Mike on the stairs. "It came from our room."

He followed me up, and we met the kids in the upper hall. Jerry looked scared, and Freddie's big blue eyes were full of tears.

"It hit me," Freddie said. He held out his arm, and there was a red welt across the back of his hand.

I glanced past him and didn't see any broken lamps or scattered model parts. "What hit you?" I demanded.

"The book," Jerry said. "He was going to pick it up, and it jumped off the desk and fell on him."

"Oh, sure," Mike said. "All our books jump up and hit you if you try to touch them when you've been told not to. My models will bite, too, so stay away from them."

I remembered the way that book had slid off the table in the library, though. I hadn't told Mike, or anyone else except Jeff, about that. I didn't want anybody to think I was crazy.

"Well, it'll leave you alone if you stay out of here," I told the kids, "so go downstairs, and don't come back up."

I looked at the book they were talking about, the dusty old dark blue one, and picked it up off the floor. Maybe I'd better get around to reading it pretty soon, I thought uneasily. It made my fingers sort of tingle, just touching it.

Once the food was ready, we all stayed outside, and I forgot about the book. When we finally went up to bed, though, Mike stopped in the doorway. "Hey! Alex, I thought you put that book on the desk."

"I did," I said. Only that wasn't where it was. It was on my bed.

Again it sort of made my fingers tingle when I set it beside the lamp on the nightstand. Probably it was only my imagination, I thought. I was too tired to look at it tonight, anyway.

Mike put on his pajamas and slid into bed. "School tomorrow. Gosh, vacation wasn't long enough, was it?"

"It never is," I said. Except for Norm Winthrop

being there, though, I didn't mind going to school again. "I'm kind of looking forward to playing soccer again. I'm glad Mr. Radwicke's going to be our coach this year. Everybody likes him."

"I hope I get Mr. Jaeger for art," Mike said sleepily. To Mike anything to do with drawing or painting was more interesting than anything athletic.

I got into bed, wishing I hadn't thought about Norm. That wiped out the anticipation I'd otherwise have had about seeing all the other kids again. Some of them came on buses, so I didn't see them through the summer.

Norm lived in town. I'd seen him twice since school got out last June. The first time was at Thrifty Foods, where he'd rammed me with a shopping cart so I'd dropped a carton of eggs. Three of them smashed. I didn't mind the eggs as much as I did the way my foot hurt where he ran over it.

The second time was in an even more public place. It was at the town picnic during the Strawberry Festival the end of June. The festival is just an excuse to get people out for special sales and entertainments. There was a parade in the morning, and then a couple of thousand people gathered in the park for the picnic. You could bring your own food, or buy stuff. Mom said she cooks enough the rest of the time, so we lined up for the salmon barbecue.

I loaded up my plate with salmon and potato salad and cole slaw and rolls; there was going to be strawberry shortcake for dessert, later. I was walking carefully through the crowd toward the table where I saw Jeff and his folks.

I didn't notice Norm. I don't know what he was

doing there; he didn't buy anything to eat. I came to a narrow place between two tables where people were already eating, and I lifted my plate up high so there'd be room to get it through without bumping anyone.

Jeff was watching, waving at me to come on, and he saw what happened. The only thing I knew was that I was carefully balancing that loaded plate up about the level of my chin, and somebody shoved hard on my elbow.

I stumbled forward, and the plate tilted; I got my footing and stared in horror as I saw my dinner dumped over the head of a woman on one of the benches. A pat of butter slid down inside the back of her dress; the salmon and the salads made a trail down her front and ended up in her lap.

The woman shrieked and jumped up. Several paper cups on the table overturned, and the punch ran onto the people on each side of her. The woman turned around and looked at me, and it was Mrs. Brezonski, the mayor's wife.

She was wearing a pale pink dress, and it was a mess. Everybody was exclaiming and jumping up to help—or to get out of the way, I don't know which—and a little girl who'd had red punch run into the lap of her white dress started to cry.

I wanted to cry myself. I wanted to crawl under a table. I wanted to kill Norm Winthrop.

He hadn't waited to see how it all came out. I saw him heading out toward the street, and I knew who'd pushed me, even before Jeff told me.

That had been months ago, but it still made my face and ears get red when I thought about it. Nobody but Jeff seemed to have seen what really happened. Everybody thought I was careless, goofing around, and my own mother said, "Oh, Alex!" as if it had been my fault.

I never did get anything to eat at the picnic. I'd lost my appetite, so that part didn't matter, but the story went around for days, how funny it had been. Funny to everybody but me and the people who got splattered with my food and the spilled punch.

Shoot, I thought. Why did I have to remember that and spoil the good things about going back to school?

I was just dozing off when I suddenly felt a blow to the head. It stunned me for a minute; and then when I put my hands up, I knew at once what it was. That confounded book had slid off the table and fallen on me. No wonder there'd been a welt on Freddie's hand. It was heavy, and it hurt.

This time I felt more than just a tingling in my hands. I felt peculiar all over, and for a minute it was hard to breathe.

There was no mistaking it. That book was moving on its own, unless we'd had an earthquake. I hadn't noticed an earthquake, though.

I reached up and turned on the light, glancing over to see that Mike was sound asleep. He didn't stir as I sat up and looked at the book beside me.

I didn't even want to touch it, but I knew I had to. Somehow, I was convinced that book *wanted* me to read it, and it wasn't going to rest until I did.

I opened the pages and saw once more my own name written in that spidery hand, and I swallowed as I began to read.

"ALEX, what are you doing with a light on at this time of night?"

I jerked upright when my dad appeared in the doorway. My heart pounded, and I looked at my alarm clock. It was after eleven.

"You have to get up early tomorrow, remember? Back to school. Come on, go to sleep, son."

"Yeah, OK," I agreed. I put the book aside and turned off the light, sliding down under the covers.

I'd read for an hour and hardly gotten started. My eyes burned, because the print was small and not very dark. My heart was pounding in my chest so I could almost hear it.

I couldn't wait to talk to Jeff in the morning.

"It's full of spells you can put on people," I said as we walked along the sidewalk toward school. "It tells you all this stuff to do, to make people do what you want, or to make something happen to them."

"You mean like sticking pins in a doll, when you've stolen someone's hair or their fingernails to put on it? So they'll hurt wherever the pin is stuck in? Voodoo, that kind of thing?"

Jeff was clearly intrigued.

"I didn't see anything that mentioned voodoo, or sticking pins in dolls. But there's some interesting stuff. The trouble is that some of the spells call for weird ingredients before you can work them. Like the eye of a newt."

"What's a newt?" Jeff asked, fascinated.

"A lizard, I think. A salamander, remember, like that one we had in second grade, in Mrs. Senecal's class?"

"Oh, yeah. How you going to get the eye of a newt?"

"I don't know. I don't think I want to kill anything

to get its parts, so I probably won't do that one. I was just giving you an example."

"What was that for? What would it do?"

"I don't remember. But there're other spells that I could probably get the ingredients for. Things like spider webs and dandelion fluff and rose petals. Aren't there still some roses over in Mrs. Critelli's yard?"

"Yeah, but they're turning brown around the edges. Will that matter?"

"I don't see why it should. On the way home let's get a few and see. And there're plenty of spider webs in the garage."

"What kind of spell are you going to do first?" Jeff wanted to know.

"I haven't decided yet. I've only read a little bit of the book, but there're spells for all kinds of things."

Jeff grinned. "See if there's one for getting me to pass my math tests this year. My dad says if I don't get at least a C average he's going to ground me."

That hadn't occurred to me. "I'll check and see. I could use some help in a few things, too. Hey, look, there's Norm Winthrop. Let's cross the street."

Norm was the same age we were, and he'd been in the same class since we were in fourth grade. Norm bullied a lot of people, but he seemed to have it in for me in particular. I never figured out why.

Once when I was talking about Norm at home, my dad asked if I was afraid of him. I tried to answer truthfully, that I didn't think I was exactly *afraid*, but I didn't like Norm. I didn't like having him shove me off the curb, or call me names, or make fun of me in front of the other kids. And those were the *mild* things he did.

I didn't see any point in starting off the year by

meeting Norm and risking a scuffle, right close to school where some of the teachers would see us. Norm was good at making adults think somebody else had started the ruckus every time he got involved in one. One reason I liked Coach Radwicke was that he didn't seem to be fooled as easily as most of the teachers.

We cut across the street, pretending we didn't see Norm.

Jeff spoke under his breath. "Are you going to try the spell for putting an end to a bully's ways?"

"I don't know. I didn't read that one yet; I don't know what you need to do it." I slid a look sideways at him. "You're talking as if you think any spell we do is actually going to work."

"I do. Don't you?" He seemed to be perfectly serious.

We were right in front of the school now, with lots of other kids around. I lowered my voice. "I don't know. There's something about that book. It's not just *about* magic, I think maybe it *is* magic. My cousin Freddie tried to pick it up, after we'd told him to stay out of our room, and it walloped him."

Jeff stopped and Cindy Higgs ran into him from behind and made a rude remark he didn't even hear. "What do you mean, it *walloped* him?"

"He said it hit him. And there was a raised red place on his hand. It hit hard enough to make him cry."

"Wow!"

This time it was Sandy Ferguson who ran into *me*.

"You're blocking the sidewalk," she said, and scowled at us.

I lowered my voice even more. "When Deidra used the book to prop up a corner of her bed, it waited until she went to sleep and then slid out of place so the bed tipped her out. And when *I* went to sleep, it jumped off the nightstand and hit me in the head. That's when I decided to read some of it."

Jeff's eyes narrowed. "Are you putting me on, Alex?"

"I swear, it's true."

For a moment he stood motionless, and then he grinned.

"When are we going to try the first spell?"

"How about after school this afternoon?" I said. I sounded confident enough, but after I'd said it, I began to have an odd sensation in the pit of my stomach. It wasn't too different from what I felt when I was alone and saw Norm Winthrop coming toward me.

"OK," Jeff agreed. "I'll go home first and change my clothes. My mom said she'd skin me if I wrecked my new jeans the first week of school, and I'm going to be careful for a few days. All right?"

I nodded, but that odd sensation didn't go away.

We found out we had Mr. Radwicke for coach and Mrs. Lowell—the oldest and grouchiest teacher in the school—for homeroom and math. Win one, lose one, as my dad says.

I kept thinking that I wanted to try one of the spells, but it was strange to be convinced that the book *wanted* me to do them.

4

A F T E R P.E., Norm shoved Bucky so he fell into a bank of lockers. It made a big racket, and Bucky hit his elbow on a bench, going down, so he got up mad enough to fight. His face was red and angry.

"Norm's the same as he was last year," I muttered to Jeff, who was toweling off after his shower.

"That's OK," Jeff replied. "We'll get him with the magic spell, right?"

Bucky took a swing at Norm and missed, and Norm laughed. Until Coach Radwicke gripped the back of his neck firmly—he's done it to me twice, so I know how firm it is—and said, "All right, Winthrop, that's enough. Go take your shower."

Norm didn't say anything, just walked past us with that grin he has that makes you want to wipe it off his face somehow. It made me feel sort of shaky, even when it wasn't me he was tormenting. Bucky had already showered, and he got dressed with his back to us.

Next time it would probably be me who got shoved into the lockers, I thought. Or off the curb, or into a wall, whenever Norm caught me off-guard. He was a real jerk.

The only friends Norm had were Jim and Don Moore; they were cousins, not brothers, and the dimwits in class. I don't think either one of them ever got any better than a C in any class, and mostly they got D's. They buttered up to Norm all the time and laughed whenever he tripped somebody. I decided that if a spell worked on Norm, I might try one on the Moores, too.

Except for that incident in the locker room, the day was pretty good. Even Mrs. Lowell was mellow, for her. She didn't assign seats, so Jeff and Bucky and I sat together in the back of the room. Maybe if we didn't horse around, she'd leave us there, we hoped.

I debated whether to include Bucky when we tried to work a magic spell. Finally I decided to keep the book a secret just between me and Jeff, at least for a while. That way, if nothing happened, only two of us would know about how foolish we were. Bucky was OK, but he wasn't the best person to keep a secret, sometimes.

When I got home, Mike was in the kitchen building a sandwich, so I made one, too. Building is the right word for Mike's sandwiches: he carefully spreads the bread with mayonnaise and mustard, then puts on layers of meat and cheese and whatever else he can find, until he has a stack so high he can barely get a corner of it in his mouth.

There was a note on the kitchen table. "Alex, check the roast and make sure it isn't getting dry, and put the potatoes in at five, please." My mom works in a hardware store and usually leaves instructions for me to do something about dinner so we can eat soon after she and Dad get home.

I swallowed a bite of peanut butter and jelly sandwich and asked Mike, "What are you going to be doing?" I didn't want him in the room when Jeff and I got going on that spell.

Mike pushed his glasses up on his nose. "I'm going over to Paul's. We're going to dissect a dead squirrel he found."

I made a face. "I hope he put it in the freezer this time, so it doesn't stink. No kidding, Mike, if you're going to share a room with me—"

"It's in the refrigerator," Mike assured me. "Don't worry. Whatever you're going to do, Alex, I won't bother you. I'll be home in time for supper."

So the house was empty except for us when Jeff came over. We took some apples up to my room and sprawled on my bed, and we opened the book.

"Let's do the spell against Norm," Jeff suggested. "What's it take? Toads and rattlesnake venom?"

"Probably. We could get the venom from a cut on Norm's finger, if we could get close enough to him to get it," I said, and we both laughed. I didn't know if I believed that anything would come of it, but if any spell would work, I wanted Norm to be the victim for a change.

The trouble was, we couldn't find the page with that particular spell on it. First I looked, and then Jeff looked, and then we looked together.

"It was there, I saw it the day you bought the book," Jeff said, puzzled.

"I saw it, too. I don't remember what it said, though.

Maybe it's in the index. What should we look under? Bullies?"

Only there was no index. You just had to go through the book page by page until you found what you wanted, and we couldn't find any mention of bullies. I was so disappointed I knew I had really believed the book would help, at least a little bit.

I sat up and dropped my apple core in the wastebasket. "Well, I guess we'll come across it again eventually. I give up for now, though. Let's see what else we can find."

Jeff flipped back to the beginning. "Hey, listen. It says, 'the spells in this book are not to be undertaken lightly by the amateur, for the consequences may be serious. Before invoking the powers conveyed by these pages, the reader should soberly consider the potential results, some of which may be irrevocable.' Do you think that means if we could make Norm walk in front of a truck he'd be killed?"

"I don't want him killed, necessarily," I said. "I just want him to stop pestering me."

"Just crippled," Jeff interpreted.

"Well, not even crippled, at least not permanently," I decided. "Just dented enough so he gets the idea that some things are painful and there are ways you can entertain yourself without making someone else miserable. But we can't do anything if we can't find that spell. How about this one?"

The one I pointed out was titled: *Spell to induce one to spend less time in profitless activity.*

"Maybe it would get Deidra out of the bathroom faster," I speculated. "She spends an hour there every morning and every night. I don't know what would be more profitless than putting all that goop around her eyes and plucking out eyebrows. I can't see where it makes her look any better. If she takes any more time in there, Mike and I will be late for school every day."

"If it works, we'll use it on *my* sisters," Jeff said. "What do we need? Any of those rose petals I swiped from Mrs. Critelli's yard? I got a whole pocketful." He dug them out, and they fluttered onto the bed and the floor.

"Rose petals, ginger, rosemary, and a touch of vinegar. Good, we ought to have all those in the kitchen except the rose petals. It doesn't say how many. Let's try half a dozen," I decided, and we went downstairs to raid the spice jars.

We stirred everything together with the vinegar. It didn't say to heat the stuff, so we just let it soak in a cup while we looked back in the book to find out how to make this spell apply to the right person. I stirred the brew with a finger while Jeff read the instructions.

" 'The completed potion should then be brought into contact with the subject in such a way that it will be absorbed through the skin.' How the heck are we going to do that?"

I had a vision of holding Deidra down and rubbing the stuff on her, but the consequences of that were probably more than I wanted to contemplate. "I don't know. Let's look in her room and see if it gives us any ideas," I said at last. "I doubt if we could get her to drink it, not with all that vinegar in it."

Deidra's bedroom wasn't very helpful. The dressing table was covered with the junk she put on her face, but we couldn't see any way to mix it with any of that. We walked back out in the hall and I glanced into the bathroom and saw a new bottle on the counter.

"Maybe that's it. Her mouthwash! She's paranoid about mouthwash; she gargles for five minutes at a time. Do you think that would be enough, if she held it in her mouth, even if she spits it out afterward? Nothing in it could hurt her."

"Unless you pour it over her, I can't think of anything better," Jeff mused. "We *could* just throw it on her when she comes in."

"And have her throw us downstairs a minute later. No, thanks. Let's try the mouthwash. Here, let's pour a little of it into that glass, and then fill the bottle with the potion."

We were laughing, kidding around, and a little of the stuff spilled on Jeff's hand. He made a big thing of washing it off very quickly, because he didn't want it to work on *him*. "I don't get the use of the bathroom enough as it is," he said. "Not with three sisters. There, it doesn't look too different, just a lighter color. Do you think she'll notice the rose petals?"

"She'll be so busy watching her own gorgeous reflection in the mirror, she won't notice a thing," I predicted.

By now it seemed silly and harmless. I didn't really believe this was going to work, not with just vinegar and spices. Except for the rose petals, wasn't that what you used to make pickles? We went downstairs, and I put the potatoes in with the roast; then we sat on the back steps and wondered how long it would take the spell to work.

"If it takes hold tomorrow morning," I said, "so I can get in and out of the bathroom in a reasonable period of time, let's leave a little early. Get to school before Norm does."

"And if it works, remember, we'll make up some more of that stuff. I wonder how much it would take for three girls? None of my sisters use mouthwash, so we'd have to trick them some other way," Jeff told me. He was still laughing when he went home for supper.

My sister came home from work at nine o'clock and went upstairs just ahead of me, so she got into the bathroom first. I sighed, looking at the closed door and the telephone cord that ran out of her room and disappeared into the bathroom. Dad had asked why she needed twenty-five feet of cord for a bedroom phone, and she had said, "I'm paying for it, Daddy, so I can carry the phone around with me. What difference does it make? It won't run up my bill, and I'm paying that, too."

I could tell him what difference it made. It meant that she could talk to Shirley while she was doing whatever it was she did in there, while I sat on the top steps of the stairs and waited for her to come out.

Before I sat down, though, I banged on the closed door and yelled. "Hurry up, I want to go to bed!"

I didn't expect any results except that Diedra would yell back, the way she usually did.

I didn't expect a scream, and then the door flying open and my sister, soaking wet and with her hair plastered to her head instead of curling the way it usually did, running out with her mouth wide open, still screaming.

I didn't have to ask why she was screaming. Aside from her hair being a mess, the evidence was plain enough.

In the bathroom the handle was broken off the cold

water faucet of the sink, and water was squirting half-way to the ceiling and running all over the floor.

In the sink lay the plastic bottle of mouthwash, where she'd dropped it. A limp bit of pink rose petal, edged in brown, stuck to the side of the sink where the water wasn't spraying.

I swallowed, surveying the mess, hearing Dad's heavy footsteps on the stairs behind me. This wasn't quite the way I'd imagined the spell would work, but Deidra sure hadn't wasted much time in the bathroom. I had to admit that.

5

"DID anything happen at your house last night?" I asked as Jeff came trotting across the corner next morning.

We fell into step and headed toward school, and he gave me a searching look.

"Depends on what you mean by happen. Wendy got locked in the bathroom somehow, and Dad made me quit watching TV and climb in the bathroom window. Only I couldn't get it unlocked, either, so eventually *he* climbed in the window, too, and nearly got stuck there. We had to take the door off the hinges to get it open. Boy, was Dad disgusted."

Wendy was his seven-year-old sister. I reflected on this. "It didn't exactly keep you out of the bathroom," I said.

He knew immediately what I meant. "Hey, I only spilled a little of that stuff on me, and I washed it right off. Besides, that spell didn't specifically say it would keep people from wasting time in the bathroom, remember? It said *to spend less time in profitless activity*. Getting the door off the hinges so we could get Wendy out without carrying her across the roof and down the ladder wasn't exactly profitless activity."

"No," I agreed thoughtfully. "But maybe watching TV was, which is what you'd been doing when the door got stuck shut. What were you watching?"

Jeff replied slowly. "An old comedy, kind of a stupid one."

I nodded, and he stopped walking and grabbed my arm. "OK, Alex, what happened at *your* house last night?"

I told him. "We had a broken faucet. Deidra said the mouthwash tasted funny. She spit it out and knocked the bottle over, then hit the faucet with her hand, trying to keep the bottle from spilling. Dad said that wouldn't have broken it, it must have been about ready to come apart, anyway. So nobody suspected anything, but she was sure mad." I ended up with, "I stirred that stuff with a finger, remember? And *I* didn't get to spend any time in the bathroom, either. Dad had the water shut off until he could fix the faucet, and nobody got any showers."

"Taking a shower isn't exactly profitless activity. Not if you want anyone to get close to you," Jeff pointed out. "What would you have been doing while Deidra was in there, if the faucet hadn't broken?"

"Sitting on the top of the stairs, waiting for my turn," I admitted. What could be more useless than that?

We looked at each other and then started walking again. I thought Jeff felt as peculiar as I did. But I still wasn't *really* convinced that the magic book had been responsible for those events.

After all, life is full of minor catastrophes even without magic spells.

As if he were reading my mind, Jeff said, "I broke my arm once without any help from your magic book. And our bathroom door has jammed like that before. I had to climb in the window, and I got it open from inside."

"Yeah," I agreed. "Deidra's bed fell down of its own accord before we worked any spells. And that faucet wasn't the first mess we ever had with the plumbing. Remember, last spring, when a pipe broke and flooded the basement? We didn't have anything to do with that."

"Sometimes you just have bad luck," Jeff decided. "Like now. We aren't early enough to miss good old Norm."

My heart sank. Norm was ahead of us, standing talking to Jim and Don Moore. They all smirked at us as we approached.

"It'll be pretty obvious we're chicken if we cross the street now," Jeff muttered under his breath.

"I'm not chicken," I objected. "It just seems stupid to get close enough to a shark so it can sink its teeth into you. Hey," I raised my voice so it would carry to the trio ahead of us, "there's Bucky. Bucky, wait up!"

I stepped off the curb before we got to Norm and the Moores, heading for Bucky on the opposite side of the street, and Jeff trotted along behind me.

I got a glimpse of Norm's grin and knew my strategy hadn't fooled him. He knew perfectly well why we weren't getting any closer to him. He waved a lazy hand and called out. "We'll let you by, Alex, you and Jeff. You don't have to be afraid of us."

We ignored him, and heard the Moores snicker. "I hope we can find that spell in the book again," I said as we reached the far side of the street.

Bucky was waiting for us, glaring at the enemy, but he was distracted by the words he'd overheard. "What are you talking about? What spell? What book?"

I hadn't really intended to tell him, but I hadn't thought before I spoke in front of him. I explained as we went on toward school.

Bucky was impressed. "No kidding, you mean you tried one spell and it really worked?"

"Well, we don't know for sure," I had to concede. "But after we did the one on Deidra, she didn't waste much time in the bathroom, and Jeff and I didn't get to waste any, either."

Bucky has an old fashioned short haircut; his reddish hair sticks straight up like one of those brushy mats designed to wipe the mud off your feet. His freckles stand out when his face gets either flushed or pale; right now he was pale, and his blue eyes were wide with excitement.

"You think you can use magic on Norm? What are you gonna make him do? Fall in the creek? Break his neck on the monkey bars? Fracture a leg when we all pile on him in football?"

"All I want is for him to stay away from me," I said, but Jeff was already elaborating on Bucky's ideas.

"Maybe he could fall in a manhole that had the cover left off."

"And then he'd sue the city for negligence and some poor innocent workman would lose his job," I objected. I knew Jeff was kidding, but it made me a little bit uncomfortable anyway. What if any of it really happened? I didn't want to be responsible for a genuine catastrophe, not even to Norm.

"What kind of spells can you do?" Bucky wanted to know.

"There's all kinds," Jeff told him. "You ought to hear some of the stuff it takes—newt's eyes and dead mice and strange herbs. Maybe you can help us find some of them."

"What does it take to stop somebody like Norm?"

"Well," I said reluctantly, "we don't remember. We only noticed the heading when I first got the book; we never read it all. And we can't find that part again. But we will."

Bucky was fascinated.

By that time we'd reached school, and at the last minute before we went in, Norm and the Moores blocked our way, grinning those mean grins.

We stopped. My heart was pounding—in anger, not in fear, I told myself.

"Get out of the way," Bucky said, attempting to go around them. But Don moved so that all the doors were covered.

"Who's going to make us?" Norm wanted to know.

A deep voice spoke behind them as Mr. Jaeger, the art teacher, pushed open a door; Norm had to move aside or get knocked over. "Don't block the doors, please, boys. There goes the first bell, break it up."

He stood holding the door open, and we all moved quickly through it. I was relieved, but ashamed, too. A teacher had solved the problem, not me. A look at Norm's face, with that familiar hateful smile, showed me he was well aware of how I felt. There were no teachers in sight now. He stuck out a foot as I went past him and sent me sprawling in the hallway.

He was gone, laughing loudly, before I could get up.

"You hurt, Alex?" Bucky asked.

"No," I lied. One elbow felt as if it had been struck

by a sledge hammer. "But I'm getting mad. I don't have to take this from him."

I'd have to find that spell, I thought. I'd look through the book again, page by page, and see what I had to do to put a stop to Norm's bullying.

If I didn't, I'd never make it through junior high.

The trouble was, when I sat down with the magic book that afternoon and went through it page by page—being careful not to leak taco sauce onto it from my warmed-up burrito—I couldn't find any section headed *Spell to put an end to a bully's ways.*

It just seemed to have disappeared from the book.

6

I T was Friday afternoon before Jeff and Bucky got over to my house so we could try another spell, and then it was late, because we all got kept after school.

It happened because when I came to math class Norm was sitting in my seat.

Bucky was standing by the teacher's desk; he gave me a look as soon as I entered the room, so I knew something was wrong even before I headed toward my seat.

Norm grinned at me, and a knot formed in the pit of my stomach. It was too much to hope for that Mrs. Lowell would notice he'd taken my seat and make him move. I hadn't figured out if the teachers really didn't see the things that Norm did, or if they pretended not to, just to avoid a confrontation.

Well, I thought sourly, as the knot burned inside me, didn't I do the same thing? I didn't want a confrontation, either, because I'd probably lose it.

Bucky followed me from the front of the room, and

I saw that Jim Moore was in *his* seat, and his cousin was in Jeff's. Bucky and Jeff, who were already there, were watching to see what I was going to do.

My mouth felt dry, and the rest of me felt shaky. I wanted to grab Norm and throw him on the floor, but I knew I wasn't going to try that. Not in front of a whole class, and have Norm maybe shove me through a window, even if the window was on the ground floor.

There were empty seats ahead of the interlopers, so I sat down in front of Norm. It was all I could think of to do, with Mrs. Lowell up front tapping her ruler for the class to come to order.

Jeff and Bucky, looking as relieved and ashamed as I felt, took seats, too, and Mrs. Lowell started writing problems on the blackboard for us to copy.

The trouble was that Norm wasn't satisfied with what was clearly his victory. After about two minutes he started poking me with his pencil. At first it wasn't painful, just little prods. When I ignored him, the pokes got harder. Pretty soon he put that sharp pencil between my shoulder blades and leaned on it until I thought maybe it was going to break the skin right through my shirt.

The knot in my stomach hadn't entirely gone away when I sat down, and now it was like a hot rock. I wondered if my legs would hold me if I stood up, because they were shaking.

The pressure on my back increased, and I heard Jim giggle very softly. It hurt, it really hurt, and Mrs. Lowell didn't seem to notice a thing. It was *her* job to maintain discipline in her classroom, and she didn't pay any attention.

I leaned forward against the desk, as far from Norm

as I could get. He leaned forward, too, keeping up the pressure, and all of a sudden I lunged sideways, out into the aisle.

I heard the pencil snap; and Norm, taken off guard, sort of fell forward, too. Somehow, when I was whirling around trying to keep from falling on my face in the aisle, my elbow caught him in the nose. Hard.

"Boys! What is going on back there?"

I hardly heard her. My pulse was pounding in my ears, my knees felt the way they did when somebody'd kicked me in the stomach during P.E.

Blood spurted from Norm's nose, all over the paper on which he'd been supposed to be copying the math problems. He grabbed for a handkerchief and held it to his face; it turned bright red almost instantly.

"Alexander Graden," Mrs. Lowell practically screeched. "Go to Mr. Hamilton's office at once!"

I caught a glimpse of Jeff's white face, and Bucky's with the freckles standing out like spattered paint. "Norm shoved me out of my seat," I said unsteadily. "He was poking a pencil into my back."

Mrs. Lowell's pursed lips didn't soften. "I told you to go to the office, Alex. I will not have rowdiness in my classroom. Norman, go to the nurse's office and get that nosebleed under control."

I saw Jeff's adam's apple bob before he spoke. "It's true, Mrs. Lowell. Norm was jabbing a pencil into Alex's back."

"Yes, he was," Bucky affirmed. "I saw it, too."

Mrs. Lowell's jaws clenched, and she smacked the ruler on the edge of her desk with a sickening sound. She'd been known to strike people's hands. "All right. All of you go to the office. You, Jeff Saul, and Sherman

Dollman. Report to Mr. Hamilton at once. And all of you are to report back here at three o'clock to do the work you should have been doing in this class."

Angry and resentful but resigned, we left the room. It wasn't fair, it wasn't fair at all, because Norm had started it, and my hitting his nose was an accident, though I certainly wasn't sorry.

Norm glared at me over the stained handkerchief, and for once I had the courage to say to him what I thought.

"I hope it's broken," I said, and turned toward the principal's office while he went toward the nurse's office in the other direction.

Mr. Hamilton was usually fairly reasonable, though he made it plain that it annoyed him to have kids sent out of class. He said he had plenty of other things to do and no time for senseless horseplay. I didn't feel this fell into that category, but I never got a chance to say so.

He was just leaving his office for a meeting and he waved us toward his secretary.

"Whatever it is, I can't listen to it now. Mrs. Walker, have them sit in my office until the bell rings, and then they can go."

"But we didn't do anything wrong," I blurted out, feeling that we at least deserved the opportunity to explain what had happened.

Mr. Hamilton didn't answer but hurried through the doorway with his briefcase.

"So much for justice," Bucky said, looking after him.

Mrs. Walker gave us a cool, though not hostile, look. "In the office, please. I hope there won't be any further fighting."

"There hasn't been any fighting," Jeff protested. "Even if there had been, after Norm practically jabbed a pencil through Alex's back, it would have been justifiable. Self-defense."

A faint smile touched the secretary's mouth. "I'm sorry. I can't change Mr. Hamilton's orders."

So we sat there watching a fly crawl up and down the window of the principal's office, and I didn't know who I disliked more, Mrs. Lowell or Norm. I thought it was a draw.

I liked the teacher even less during the time we sat in her room after school. It was all I could do to think about copying the problems, let alone working out the answers. Jeff tried to tell her, again, that what had happened had been Norm's fault, not ours, but Mrs. Lowell wouldn't listen.

Her mouth had two expressions: either it was all bunched up like a prune, or it flattened out in a straight line that looked as if it had never softened enough to smile. Today it was the flat straight line, and she sounded meaner than a junkyard dog.

"We will not discuss this further, Jeffrey. I'm giving you the opportunity to make up the work you would otherwise have missed. If you prefer to go home and take a failing grade on this paper, you may do that instead. But I will not argue with you over your behavior earlier today."

Yeah, I definitely didn't like her any better than I liked Norm, I thought, and tried to concentrate on the math paper.

Mike was toasting himself a cheese sandwich when I got home, and I talked him into making me one, too, as long as he had the electric griddle hot. "You going over

42

to Paul's again?" I asked while I got out apples to go with the sandwiches.

"Yeah. We're going to work with that squirrel again. It's getting sort of ripe, even in the refrigerator, so this is probably the last time we'll be able to do it. What're you going to do?"

"Oh, nothing special," I said casually. After he'd gone I went upstairs and opened the magic book on my desk while I ate. It was crazy that I couldn't find the spell I wanted most to work, when I knew it had to be there somewhere. Jeff and I had both seen it.

My second choice, I decided, would be something to make Mrs. Lowell aware of how unfair life could be, though since she'd probably never connect it with her refusal to listen to Bucky and Jeff and me, it wasn't likely to teach her a lesson.

We were all sitting around talking about it—Bucky and me sprawled on the beds while Jeff sat at the desk leafing through the pages of the book—when Mike showed up. He poked at his glasses to push them higher on his nose.

"Hi. What're you doing?"

"Talking," I said. "How come you're home? I thought you'd be at Paul's until suppertime."

Mike shrugged. "Mrs. Sandifer said maybe I'd better go home."

We all stared at him.

"How come? What did you do?"

"I didn't do anything." Mike peeled off his sweater and dropped it on the foot of his bed. He looked little and skinny without it. "Mrs. Sandifer accidentally got the dead squirrel Paul had stored in the plastic bag instead of the cold roast she thought it was. She got hysterical when she dumped it on a plate and sent me home. Paul says she'll get over it. She did when we froze the skunk."

Bucky's mouth was hanging open. "Why are you freezing skunks and refrigerating squirrels?"

"To examine them," Mike told him. He sounded like a patient teacher explaining to a backward student. "We draw them so they look real."

Bucky made a retching sound, leaning over the edge of the bed. "I don't blame Paul's mom for getting upset. Yuk!"

"I'm going over to the playground," Mike said. "We're going to get up a ballgame."

We listened to his footsteps on the stairs, and then Bucky said, "Your little brother is weird, Alex, do you know that?"

I didn't have to answer because Jeff suddenly stopped flipping pages and kept his finger on the middle of one of them.

"Here. Here's one, let's try this."

"What is it?"

He read it slowly. *"Spell to bring attention to an injustice so that it may be righted.* Don't you think Mrs. Lowell ought to be made aware that she's done Alex—and Bucky and me, too—an injustice?"

I sat up and leaned forward. "What does it say the spell will take?"

Jeff read off the list with satisfaction. "An owl's feather, a holly berry, three hairs from the beard of a redheaded man, and the bone from a chicken leg. We ought to be able to get all of those before Monday, don't you think?"

"Where?" Bucky asked, sounding bewildered.

"Where are we going to find a holly berry this time of year? It's too early," I said.

Jeff was reading the list again. "Who do we know who has a red beard?"

"There's an owl lives in that old barn behind my grandpa's," Bucky contributed. "There's bound to be a feather or two under it. And we'll probably have chicken on Sunday when we go there for dinner. I'll get a bone out of a leg."

"What about the holly, though, and the redheaded man?"

"Alex, you give up too easy. We haven't even tried yet," Jeff said. "We've got an artificial Christmas wreath that has holly berries on it."

"Real berries? Or artificial ones?"

"I don't know. I suppose they're artificial. That might not matter, though. It doesn't specify that they have to be *real*. After all, why think up a spell that only works around Christmas time when the holly berries are ripe? We could try it that way, anyhow."

"So all we have to do is get the red whiskers," I said, sounding a bit sarcastic.

Jeff closed the book. "Right. I'll get the holly berries, Bucky will get the owl feather and the chicken bone, and you can get the red whiskers, Alex. Then we'll get together Sunday evening, OK? Everybody do their homework ahead of time, so nobody will care if we meet after Bucky gets home from his grandpa's."

I snorted in exasperation. "How the heck am I supposed to get the red whiskers? I don't know anybody who has a red beard."

"There are twelve thousand people in this town," Jeff pointed out. "You ought to be able to find someone with a red beard." He got up. "It's time I went home. We're having hot dogs tonight, and I want to be on time, or there won't be any left."

Jeff punched me lightly on the arm. "Try, huh, Alex?"

I sighed. "OK, I'll try," I agreed.

"W ho do you know who has a red beard?" I asked Mike at last, after I'd gone over, in my mind, everybody I could think of.

He was painting a ship model; I didn't know the name of it, but it was a beautiful sailing ship. For a kid his age, he was pretty good; he was slow and careful and kept the paint where it was supposed to be.

"Goober," he said, not looking up at me.

"Huh?"

"Goober. The old guy who runs the dump."

"Goober? Is that his name?"

"I don't know what his name is. He's always eating peanuts, so they call him Goober." Mike dipped the tiny brush into the gilt paint and carefully wiped off most of it on the edge of the bottle.

"Oh, yeah. There's some old song about eating goober peas. I guess they're peanuts. The dump, huh? It's open on Saturday, isn't it?"

He didn't answer that time. He was absorbed in some very delicate work with the paint brush, and after a minute I went away.

The dump was out beyond the city limits. I rode my bike, wondering all the way how I was going to get three hairs from this Goober's beard when I got there. You don't just walk up to a stranger and ask for some of his whiskers, not without taking a risk. It was only the thought of Mrs. Lowell and Norm that kept me pedaling.

It was a nice day, and it was a pleasant ride. The leaves were turning yellow and red on the oaks and vine maples; there was an Indian summer haze in the air, and the smell of bonfires where people were cleaning up their yards before winter came.

I always thought the dump was a fascinating place. When we were younger, about Mike's age, Jeff and Bucky and I went out there sometimes and just prowled around, looking at all the stuff people had thrown away. In those days they didn't keep you out, or charge you to dump, and if you found something you wanted, you just took it. Once I found a perfectly good jackknife; I carried it for several years before I lost it.

Now you had to pay to dump, and if you wanted anything anybody else had left, you had to negotiate with the dump tender for it; you couldn't just take it away. We didn't go out there anymore.

For a minute I wondered what I was doing here, getting stuff for a spell on Mrs. Lowell when all that really mattered was finding a way to stop Norm from ruining my life. He *was* ruining a lot of things for me, both in school and out of it. I could picture myself spending years more of torture and having Norm trip me on graduation day when I walked across the platform to get my diploma, probably so I'd fall off into the audience and break my leg.

For some reason I suddenly remembered once when my grandpa told me about how he'd dashed into a burning building and rescued an old lady in a wheelchair before the fire trucks got there; I'd asked him how he'd worked up the courage to do it. I couldn't think of anything more terrifying than deliberately running into a fire.

"Weren't you scared?" I asked.

"Scared to death," Grandpa said, nodding.

"Then how did you make yourself do it?"

Grandpa looked at me thoughtfully. "Well, Alex," he said finally, "*not* doing it, letting Mrs. Berlin burn to death, would have been worse than going in there after her. Do you understand? When what needs to be done is more important than being afraid to do it, you get brave enough to act. That's what bravery is, you know: being afraid, but acting, anyway, because it's the right thing to do."

I didn't quite see how that applied to my situation with Norm, though, so why was I remembering it now? If Norm started something, and I stood up to him, he'd probably finish it, too. Staying away from him seemed more sensible than getting beaten up.

I slowed down as I approached the little hut where the dump tender sat. It wasn't much bigger than a telephone booth, and this Goober had a seat in there. He was reading a paperback book that looked as if he'd salvaged it from someone's trash, and at first he didn't notice me as I stood before the open window.

He had a red beard, all right, It was getting streaked with gray, like the hair on his head, but it was still red enough to qualify for the spell, I thought. My heart began to hammer as I tried to think, at the last minute, how to go about this.

He looked up, then, and smiled. "Morning," he said.

"Morning." My mouth had a way of going dry when I was uncertain of how to handle something.

"Have a peanut?" He had them in a little bowl, and he pushed it toward me in a friendly way. I took a few, just to return the friendliness. "Full of nutrition, peanuts are. High in protein. Taste good, too."

I was chewing, so I didn't have to reply quite yet.

"Nice day, ain't it?" Goober said. "Everybody hauling things to the dump. Bags full of leaves they don't want to burn, cleaning out their garages and attics. Don't get as much of that stuff as we used to, you know. People have yard sales, now, instead of throwing their junk away. But we still get some interesting items from time to time. Last feller, now, he emptied a load of bottles been in his basement for fifty years. People collect bottles. Some of 'em are valuable. You know anybody collects bottles?"

I swallowed the peanuts. "No, sir," I said.

He helped himself to some of the nuts. "What can I do for you, son?"

And the idea came to me then. "I—I'm on a scavenger hunt. I have to collect a bunch of things and get back first with them," I said. It was *almost* true.

He chuckled. "That so? I went on a scavenger hunt, once. Didn't win it, though. I needed an argyle sock, and I couldn't find anybody had one. What is it you're needing, boy?"

I inhaled and hoped he wouldn't be insulted. "I need three hairs from the beard of a redheaded man."

For a moment he was astonished, and then he threw back his head and laughed.

"Well, you come to the right place, that you did! Three hairs, eh?" He tugged at his beard. "Might have to hunt to make sure you got three *red* ones. They're going gray at a terrible rate. Beard's grayer than my head. Sure you don't want some of these?" He touched a lock that fell over his forehead.

"No, sir, it specified from a beard."

"How they going to tell the difference?" he asked, but to my relief, he dug a pocketknife from his pants and hacked off a little clump of the brushy beard. "Here, that ought to be plenty. Let me see, you should have something to carry it in or you're going to lose it." He groped around his feet and came up with a grease-stained paper bag. "I'll take my lunch out of this, and you can use this sack. There, how's that?"

"It's great," I told him sincerely. "Thank you very much."

So now, if Jeff and Bucky came through, we had what we needed for the spell.

I WAS sitting on the porch steps waiting when Jeff showed up late Sunday afternoon. "I got the holly berries," he said, displaying them on the palm of his hand.

I looked at them critically. "The spell may not work with artificial ones, you know."

"They look real," Jeff argued. "There aren't any real ones available right now, so what will it hurt to try them?"

I shrugged. "Here comes Bucky. If he's got the

owl's feather and the chicken bone, I guess we can start working up the spell on Mrs. Lowell and see. It's too bad the book doesn't give us some idea of what's actually going to happen. I mean, having water spray all over her from a broken faucet, like what happened to Deidra, might serve her right for being so unreasonable. But it won't teach her any lesson, will it? She'd just think it was an accident, and it might make her even more disagreeable than she already is. Hi, Bucky. You get everything?"

He was puffing from running. "Well, I got the feather. I brought some extras in case any of the other spells call for some more. But I didn't get the bone. Grandma cooked ham, I don't know why; she *always* has fried chicken when we go out there. Until this time."

"Then we can't do the spell," Jeff said, scowling. "I was counting on doing it tonight."

"You get the hairs from a red beard, Alex?" Bucky wanted to know.

"From the old guy at the dump, the one they call Goober," I said, displaying my paper bag with the beard clippings in it.

Jeff looked inside. "Looks more gray than red," he commented.

"We only need three red ones, and there's that many," I assured him. "Well, I guess we just have to wait until somebody has chicken so we can get the bone."

Bucky sank down onto the step beside me. "I was hoping maybe someone else had had chicken. Is there any other spell we can do, one that doesn't need a chicken bone?"

Jeff was already perking up, dropping the holly berries back into his pocket. "How about something to help me pass the math test Monday, Alex? Let's see if there's anything in the book for that."

So we went upstairs and got out the book, and I started looking through it, with Jeff and Bucky looking over my shoulder. "Here, how about this one? *A spell for excellence in an intellectual competition.* Would that cover it?"

"It isn't a competition," Bucky protested, "it's just an old math test."

"It *is* a competition, in a way," Jeff said thoughtfully. "Mrs. Lowell marks on the curve, so if you have one of the highest scores, even if it isn't perfect, you could get an A. You *are* competing against the rest of the class."

"And it's intellectual," I added.

Bucky was looking disappointed. "But Jeff studied his math. I know he did, because I tried to call him this afternoon to tell him I couldn't get the chicken bone, and his Mom said she couldn't interrupt him because he had to finish studying before he could talk to me. So what'll it prove, if he passes the test? He'll probably pass it anyway."

For a moment there was silence, and then Jeff's face brightened. "I know how to do it. Who's the dumbest guy in sixth grade, as far as math is concerned?"

Bucky and I spoke in a chorus. "Jim Moore."

Jeff grinned. "Right. So if we put a spell on Jim, too, to pass the test, we'll know if it worked or not, won't we?"

Bucky drew in a long breath. "You think you can make a spell that will make Jim get a good grade in a math test?"

"Well, if he does, it'll prove the spell worked,

won't it? Let's try it and see. What does it take for that one, Alex?" I ran a finger across the page, following the directions, but Bucky interrupted.

"If you're going to prove anything, you'll have to have Jim get a really good grade. I mean, say what it has to be, ahead of time."

"OK," Jeff agreed. "He usually gets D's and F's. Let's say he'll have to have a C."

"He might accidentally get a C," Bucky pointed out. "Make it a B. I don't remember Jim ever getting a B in anything."

We agreed on that, and set out to round up the ingredients. They were all things we found in our house—an eyelash, it didn't say from whom, a fish scale (my dad had caught a couple of bass that weekend, and they were still in the refrigerator because there hadn't been enough to feed the whole family) and some herbs that my mom kept in little jars.

The only trouble with the spell was that you had to saturate a piece of cloth or paper with the resulting concoction, and it had to be carried or touched by the person the spell was to affect.

"How we going to get Jim to touch or carry anything?" Bucky wanted to know. Jim would be suspicious if we even spoke to him, let alone handed him anything.

"We'll think of something, before the test," I assured them, and we decided that just to be on the safe side, it wouldn't hurt anything if Bucky and I tried the spell, too. A B grade for each of us, as well as Jim, would almost have to be the result of a miracle.

W H E N we did the spell to get my sister out of the bathroom, we'd just mixed up the solution and put it in her mouthwash bottle, and it had looked perfectly ordinary.

Still, I thought it had worked, so this time we put the ingredients together very carefully. Only it wasn't quite so ordinary.

There wasn't much liquid, for one thing. I measured out the herbs and six drops of water into a small bowl, and Bucky dropped in the fish scale. I stirred those together, and then Jeff held out the eyelash and let it flutter into the mixture.

A wisp of smoke rose from the bowl.

We stared at each other, startled. Smoke? From herbs and water and an eyelash and a fish scale?

I forgot to stir in the eyelash. "It stinks," I said.

Jeff and Bucky were already wrinkling their noses. "I'll say," Bucky agreed. "Wow! If we try to get close to anybody with this, they're going to notice it."

Tentatively, I dipped my spoon into the concoction

and stirred. The smell got worse, and the smoke drifted up again, a little puff of it. It made me feel peculiar. I guess the other guys felt funny, too. Nobody said anything for a minute. We stood around the table and watched that mixture as it formed a bubble that broke, making about the worst smell I ever smelled, and then there was nothing more. It just sat there.

I drew in a long breath. "It looks and smells as if it ought to do something," I said finally. "What'll we put it on?"

The best thing we could find to soak up the solution was a bookmark. Four of them, actually. I took them out of some paperbacks my dad had brought home; our bookshop puts one in each copy, for advertising. I dipped out the stuff and dribbled it on the bookmarks.

Bucky was dubious about using bookmarks. "Jim never reads anything. And he's going to know the bookmark doesn't belong to him. He'll just throw it away, even if you manage to get it into his math book."

"You got any better ideas?" Jeff asked. "It doesn't say how long he has to be in contact with it, so even if he takes it out of his book and throws it away, he'll have to handle it. Maybe," he added, laughing, "long enough to get a C, anyway."

"It has to be a B, or the spell didn't work," Bucky insisted. "It'd be better if it was something of his own."

"Sure. Only how you going to get anything of his own? Can you imagine walking up to him, while he's standing around with Don and Norm, and asking him for a handkerchief or a paper he's working on?"

We saw Jim on the way to school, but he was with his buddies, and we didn't want to risk starting anything by getting close to them. I was the one carrying his bookmark, and several people gave me looks that made me think they thought I didn't bathe often enough. I couldn't wait to get the whole thing over with.

I didn't get a chance to plant the bookmark, and it was time to take the test. Jeff gave me a look that said *Go on, do it somehow.*

My mouth felt dry as I looked at Jim. He got up to sharpen a pencil, and that gave me the idea. I got up, too, before Mrs. Lowell could actually hand out the test papers, and on my way to sharpen a pencil that already had a point on it, I managed to knock Jim's books off his desk.

They landed with a sound like an explosion. Mrs. Lowell glared at me, and I said, "Sorry, they were sticking over the edge of the desk," and hoped she'd accept that. When I bent to pick up the books, I shoved the marker between the pages of his math book.

Norm was watching me thoughtfully, eyes narrowed, so I went and ground a quarter of an inch off my pencil and retook my seat.

I worked steadily through my own paper. I wasn't really worried about my mark, I never got less than a passing grade, and I *had* studied for the test.

When I finished, I glanced over at Jim. He was chewing on the eraser end of his pencil, his lank hair falling over his forehead. Then he took the pencil out of his mouth and began to work a problem. I couldn't see what he was writing, but it was on the second page of the test, so he'd nearly finished.

Jeff caught my eye and grinned. Bucky was still working.

"Time," Mrs. Lowell said. "Sherman, will you collect the papers, please?"

For a minute Bucky didn't react. I think sometimes he actually forgets his name is Sherman. When she repeated his name, though, he sprang up and began to gather the tests to carry forward.

Tomorrow she'd give them back to us, graded, and we'd see how the spell had turned out.

T H A T afternoon on the way home we saw Norm up to his usual tricks. He'd backed Virgil Crabb up against a light post and was poking him with a finger. Not hard enough to hurt, just enough to be humiliating.

"Someone ought to punch him out," Bucky muttered, but he didn't make any move to do it.

Jim and Don were standing back watching, and some other kids had gathered, too. Virgil is a little skinny kid, but he's no coward. His face was red, and even his ears, and he struck out at Norm's hand.

"Cut it out, Winthrop," he said angrily. "Leave me alone."

"You gonna make me?" Norm taunted, poking again. This time it looked to me as if he poked harder.

My mouth had this way of going dry when I was upset or angry. I was ashamed that I didn't quite have what it took to grab Norm and shove him off the curb, into the gutter where he belonged. The fact that nobody else was interfering either didn't help the way I felt about myself.

Virgil tried to step to one side just as Norm shoved again, this time with his whole hand, and Virgil went sprawling. He scrambled up and came at Norm in a fury; for a few seconds they scuffled, and the sound of blows was sickening.

When blood spouted from Virgil's lip, Norm stepped away, smiling. "Come on, guys, let's go, let the baby wipe his mouth," he said, and the Moore cousins followed him off down the street.

Virgil stood pressing a handkerchief against his mouth. He looked as shamed as I felt. For a minute everybody else stood around saying nothing, and then they began to drift away.

I felt compelled to say something to let Virgil know I was on his side. "He's a real jerk. One of these days he's going to get what's coming to him."

"I hope so," Virgil said, sounding muffled through the bloody handkerchief. He picked up his books and walked away, and I didn't feel any better.

Jeff and Bucky and I fell into step together, none of us saying anything for a while. A glance at their faces told me they felt the same way I did. We were halfway home before Jeff said, "We've got to find that spell about the bully, Alex. It must be in the book somewhere."

I had a reason to feel stronger yet about that when I got home. When I went upstairs, I heard water running in the bathroom, and then Mike came out, his wet hair sticking to his head.

"Hey! What's going on, you taking a shower this time of day?" I asked. Then I noticed that his eyes were red and puffy. He'd been crying.

The last time I saw Mike cry was when he got a car door slammed on his hand, when he was seven.

"What happened?" I asked, following him into our bedroom. He didn't look at me, and I touched his shoulder. "Come on, Mike. Tell me." There was a red scraped place on the back of his neck.

His voice was muffled. "I got stuffed in a garbage can."

For a few seconds I couldn't believe what he'd said. "You *what?*"

He did look at me, then. And even before he'd finished speaking, I felt rage building inside me.

"They did it for a joke. They stuffed me in a garbage can, outside of school. They held the lid down. Everybody laughed."

Everybody laughed. I knew what that was like.

I choked on the question, even though I already knew the answer. "Who? Who did that to you?"

Mike's lips trembled, and he pressed them together for a moment before he replied. "Norm Winthrop and the Moores. Norm, mostly. He's the one who held the lid on, so I was afraid I wouldn't be able to breathe. Jim finally made him get off."

I could hardly speak. My hands knotted into fists so my knuckles turned white. "We'll report him—"

Mike shook his head. "No. That'll just make it worse. Don't tell anybody, Alex. Next time he'll do something really terrible."

He was probably right, though that didn't make me feel any better about it. In fact, I felt awful when it dawned on me that maybe Norm was showing his contempt for me, by picking on my little brother.

If I found that spell about the bully, I thought, I'd do the very worst thing I could possibly do to Norm.

But when I went through the magic book again, looking for it, I still couldn't find it.

W E were pretty tense by the time Mrs. Lowell handed back our tests.

Jeff got his first, and held it up so the big red A showed. He twisted around so Bucky could see it, too.

Then I got mine, and the grade was B-plus. Behind Mrs. Lowell's back, I held it up so the other two could read the grade. Norm was scowling over his and I read his grade upside-down: a C-minus. I could hardly stand to look at him; he made me want to throw up.

When Bucky and Jim got theirs, and Mrs. Lowell headed for the front of the room, Jeff hissed at Bucky. "What did you get?"

"B-minus," Bucky murmured. He usually got C's.

We all turned toward Jim Moore. He had his head bent and his hands over his paper so we couldn't read the red letter on it.

"The grades on this test reflect the amount of preparation each of you put into your studying," Mrs. Lowell said, turning to face the class. "Even those students who normally do less than satisfactory work will find that studying has paid off in higher than usual scores. I hope that all of you whose grades rose on this test will continue to work at keeping them high. I'm proud of those who worked hard to pull up their grades. One paper, in particular, gives *me* considerable satisfaction."

She was looking toward the back of the room, and after a few seconds I realized she was looking at Jim Moore. "One student came to me after school last week and admitted that he did not understand the kind of problems we had been working. I did my best to make them clear, and obviously that student went home and studied extensively, because today, for the first time ever, Jim Moore earned a B."

When everybody turned around and looked at Jim, he got bright red. It wasn't the kind of embarrassment that you feel when you drop your slice of cake in your lap at a church supper, but the kind you get for praise when you aren't used to it. I couldn't remember anybody ever praising Jim for anything before.

"Wow," Bucky murmured.

"Congratulations," Jeff said, his eyes sparkling as he swung from Jim to me.

"Yeah, good work," I agreed.

Jim looked confused but happy. His cousin Don looked stupefied. He'd known Jim all his life, and he probably didn't remember anybody ever praising Jim, either.

Bucky could hardly wait until we got outside and had a chance to talk. "If he asked for help, and he went home and studied, then it wasn't because of the spell," he said.

"How do you know that? He never asked for help before. He probably never studied before," Jeff pointed out.

"The spell could have made him do those things," I added.

"We didn't stick the bookmark in his book until yesterday," Bucky said stubbornly. "He asked for help and studied before that."

"I still think we're the ones who caused it, with the spell." It was going to take a lot to convince Jeff differently.

"What's going to happen," Bucky asked, "if Jim can't keep on doing B work? We going to keep doing spells for him every time we have a test? Even if he is a buddy of Norm's?"

It hadn't occurred to me that we might start something that would put the responsibility for someone else's grades onto our shoulders. I remembered how Jim had looked, earning what was probably the best grade he'd ever had in his life. He wouldn't have any way of knowing that a magic spell had earned it for him.

"Seems kind of cruel to let him go back to being the class dunce," I said uneasily.

"So what are we going to do? Repeat the spell every time there's a test? We're going to run out of eyelashes and fish scales," Bucky charged.

"Let's try something else for a test," I suggested. "Something that isn't likely to happen, and see if we can make it happen."

I didn't know what to think about those spells. Maybe the book just fell off the desk and hit Freddie's hand and off my nightstand to smack me in the head while I was sleeping and slid out from under Deidra's bed without any magic. Maybe everything would have been the same even if we hadn't done any spells at all.

"What'll we do?" Bucky asked, willing to be convinced of the magic.

"Make Norm Winthrop fall down a flight of stairs," Jeff proposed. "If he breaks a leg so he has to be in a cast and on crutches for the next six weeks, he won't be shoving anyone around for a while."

"Breaking a leg would be too good for him," I said. "Only I can't find that confounded spell."

"We could swoop up Norm and carry him away," Jeff said, "and drop him in the gravel pit. That deep part where it's full of water, so he couldn't get out."

"Look through the book and find a good spell, Alex," Bucky said when we parted company. "And let us know what to get to do it, so we can maybe do it after school tomorrow."

So when I got my brownies and milk and a banana, I carried them upstairs and settled down to go through the book one more time.

B u c k y stood at the desk, looking at the drawing Mike had left there. "Hey, you know, your little brother is getting pretty good, Alex. You see this, Jeff? I wish I could draw that good. You suppose you could magic me into being an artist with one of those spells, buddy?"

"Not even magic is that strong," Jeff objected. "You're right, though, Mike's real good at drawing." He sat down on the edge of my brother's bed. "You think it was the spell that made Jim Moore get a good grade in math?"

"He studied ahead of time," Bucky said stubbornly. "Anybody would get a better grade if they studied and asked the teacher for special help."

"How come he asked for help on this particular test," Jeff wanted to know, "when he never did before? Never studied before."

"Who knows? But I don't believe it was a spell."

"We all got good grades," I pointed out. "After we

each carried one of the bookmarks with the solution on it." I *wanted* to believe there was genuine magic; I wanted to stop Norm in his tracks.

"You and Jeff usually get passing grades."

"Sure. Jeff usually gets B's or C's, and he got an A. And you got a B, which is pretty good for you."

"Magic me into getting rich," Bucky suggested. "I already spent my allowance for this week, and I didn't pay for my student union card, so I can't go to the game Friday night. Fix me up with that, will you?"

We were just kidding around, with the suggestions getting more and more wild. We couldn't find a spell in the book that sounded as if it would make Bucky rich enough to pay for a student union card. There weren't any spells that sounded as if they'd make anybody really rich, or we'd have tried it for all of us.

"So far all the spells we've tried have been for things that were easily possible," Jeff pointed out. "Let's try for something not very likely at all."

So we sat around thinking up things that weren't very likely to happen. We kept coming up with things like Bucky making a home run when we played baseball during noon hour (he's pretty chunky and not very well coordinated; he can't run fast, so even if he hits a long ball he has trouble making it around the bases), or Jeff's room being cleaned up so he wouldn't have to spend Saturday morning doing it or me having a perfect checkup and not needing any fillings when I went to the dentist on Thursday after school.

"Well, heck," Bucky said, "let's try 'em all. What do we have to lose? Can you find spells that look like they'd do those things, Alex?"

"I can try," I agreed, reaching for the book and flipping pages. "I sure wish this thing had an index."

"Maybe you could magic it into having one," Bucky said. "Look and see."

We didn't find a way to create an index. The book probably didn't want one. I had decided the book was running the show, not us, that it would only let us do what it wanted us to. But I didn't say that to the others. It would sound crazy, even to my best friends.

We did find spells that would work for Bucky getting a home run, and Jeff's room being cleaned up so he wouldn't have to waste a perfectly good Saturday doing it, and me having a perfect checkup. They all looked easy, and we didn't have much trouble getting the stuff together to do them, except for the toenails of a wild animal.

We hesitated over that one. It was for the spell to make Bucky get the home run, and he insisted we try. He really wanted that. "Listen," he said, "hasn't your little brother got anything in the freezer that we could take the claws off? A raccoon or a squirrel, or something like that?"

"Maybe," I said, but I wasn't about to mutilate his frozen model without his permission. I was feeling rotten about Mike, afraid it was because Norm had it in for *me* that he'd gone after Mike. "I'll ask."

Mike stared at us through the glasses. "What do you want them for?"

"I'll tell you later," I said. "Can you get us some claws?"

Mike considered. "You want them from a rat? Or I can go over to Paul's and get the claws off a blue jay.

That hasn't been in the freezer, though, so it might stink."

We didn't know if a bird would be considered a wild animal or not, so we went with the rat claws. Mike was used to dissecting things, and he removed them for us. He was curious, I could see, but he didn't stick around after he'd handed them over.

We assembled the ingredients on our kitchen table, and I took a deep breath. I was almost afraid to put them together. We'd had those wisps of smoke and that terrible stench the last time. What would we get this time?

I put the things for the first spell into a dish and waited. Nothing happened. "This one's for you," I told Bucky. "You read out the magic words."

Bucky swallowed and stared into the dish. "What are they?"

I showed him in the book. Bucky's not the world's best reader, and we didn't know if he pronounced the words right, but he read them off uncertainly. Then he gulped.

The stuff in the dish began to move. Slowly, like pudding when you're mixing it on the stove and it begins to boil. It moved sluggishly, in a clockwise direction. And then it stopped.

I was sweating, and Bucky had beads of moisture on his forehead, too. "Is that all?" he asked hoarsely.

"Looks like it," Jeff decided. "Now, do mine."

He didn't sweat over his. He was supposed to drink this one, and there were no magic words to be said. He looked at the combination of herbs and weeds and spices. "I'm glad this isn't the one with the rat toenails in it," he said, and lifted the dish.

Bucky watched as if he expected flames to come out of Jeff's mouth, but all that happened was that Jeff grimaced at the taste. "Nobody'd make a fortune on that formula for a soft drink," was all he said.

The one for my dental checkup was simple, too. I didn't have to drink it, just stir it with a finger. I thought it felt warm, but maybe that was my imagination.

It was Jeff who thought up something that would "prove, one way or the other," whether or not there was genuine magic in the book.

"Let's see if we can make school close on Friday," he said. "If we didn't have school for an extra day, we'd have time to work up something really worthwhile."

"School's barely started," I said. "It's not likely we're going to get a day off already. It's too soon for parent/teacher conferences or anything like that, and there's no holiday."

"Good. Then let's try it," Bucky decided for us all.

Deidra was kind of ticked off when she found out we'd snipped a little of the fringe from the afghan she kept on the foot of her bed—it was the only source of wool we could think of, and we took such a small amount she'd never have noticed if she hadn't caught us at it. But for a few minutes I was afraid we were in trouble.

Her eyes practically shot sparks. "What do you think you're doing in my room, anyway, Alex?"

"You went in mine," I reminded her, "when you wanted to borrow a book to hold up the corner of your bed."

"That's different. I only borrowed it, I didn't damage it."

"Hey, look, it hardly shows where we took the yarn, see? Nobody'll ever notice it."

"But it's mine, not yours, and you didn't ask permission. What do you need a hunk of yarn for?"

Bucky and Jeff exchanged uneasy glances, which she didn't notice because she was so mad at me.

"Uh—we're doing an experiment. We need wool for it, and all the yarn in Mom's knitting bag says orlon or something, all synthetic. I remembered the afghan was wool because Grandma warned you about washing it in hot water and shrinking it."

For a minute I thought she was going to demand to have the little bits of yarn back, but there was no way to reattach them in the fringe so they'd look right.

"Well, from now on," she said ominously, "you stay out of my room and leave my stuff alone. Or you'll be sorry, Alex."

We had everything else we needed. We waited until Deidra went upstairs, and in silence I put things together for our final spell of the day, for the school to close on Friday.

I suppose we'd been lulled into a false sense of security by the tameness of the spells we'd just done. At least I wasn't especially apprehensive about this one. I was just wishing it was a spell to fix Norm Winthrop.

I dropped in the final ingredient—some hairs we'd got from the same rat who contributed his toenails—and read the foreign-sounding words out of the book.

This time the reaction wasn't slow and creepy, like the mess that had swirled clockwise in the dish. I hadn't even completed the final word when everything I'd put together turned a disgusting shade of green and swelled up, running over the edge of the dish and all over the table.

It smelled, as Jeff said afterward, like we'd opened up a pocket in the earth where some revolting monster lived, one that hadn't cleaned out its quarters in two hundred years.

Bucky clapped a hand over his mouth and headed for the sink. Jeff and I gulped and swallowed hard, fighting nausea.

I watched the green slime drip onto a chair and then onto the floor.

"Geeze, my mom's going to kill me," I said, choking.

"The stuff's stopped moving," Jeff observed after a moment. "I think—we better clean it up. You got any paper towels?"

Bucky was no help. Jeff and I used two rolls of towels, and carried the sopping result out to the garbage cans. My heart was racing by this time. The book *had* to be magic, I thought. But why wasn't it letting me have the spell I really wanted?

We scrubbed and scrubbed where the slime had touched anything, but there was a faint odor that lingered. When my mom came home, she paused in the middle of the kitchen and asked, "What's that smell?"

"I don't know," I said. That was the truth. There was nothing in what I'd mixed up that should have either boiled over or created such a sickening smell.

"I wonder if we've got a dead mouse in the wall or something," Mom said, frowning.

Within a few hours, though, the stink was gone. I was glad of that. I wouldn't have wanted to stand by while my mom made Dad tear the walls apart looking for a dead rodent, but I wouldn't have wanted to explain where the smell came from, either.

T H E next day, Bucky hit a home run, all right. There was an argument about whether to count it or not, because he hit the ball through a window in Soldanski's house, next door to the school, and then he just stood there and forgot to run after he heard the glass smashing.

We couldn't get the ball back, though, so finally he trotted around the bases. Then the bell rang and we went back inside. In the afternoon Mr. Hamilton interrupted class to ask about the broken window. Mrs. Soldanski had come home to find glass all over her living room rug.

"Nobody has ever hit a ball over that fence before, not in that direction," he said. "We thought when we put up the chain link fence we wouldn't be in this kind of trouble any more."

Bucky shifted uneasily in his seat. "I didn't mean to break the window. I just wanted to hit it hard enough to give me time to get around the bases."

Mr. Hamilton sighed. "Well, I guess the insurance will take care of it. But I hope it doesn't happen again."

On Wednesday, Mom made fried chicken for supper.

I took a thigh and a leg, to make sure I had the right bones, and managed to get them out of the kitchen without anyone asking me what I was doing with them. Neither Jeff nor Bucky could come over that night, because they both had to do homework. So I worked the spell against Mrs. Lowell myself with the ingredients we'd gathered before. She had bawled me out again that day for talking when I wasn't supposed to; I thought she deserved whatever this spell did to her. It was funny how she never saw Norm when he did anything to me, like putting up a foot and trying to shove me off my seat, but she always noticed when I told him to knock it off.

Anyway, I put together the stuff and said the incantation that went with it. I'll admit I was nervous, after what had happened the last time, but again it was pretty tame. All I got were a few puffs of harmless smoke.

On Thursday I had a dentist's appointment right after school. Dr. Hughes hummed to himself while he did the examination, and I hoped that meant he was pleased that my teeth were in good shape, not that he was happy he was going to make money on a dozen fillings. It was hard not to be tense while I waited to hear.

"Well, Alex," he announced when he finally pushed the overhead light to one side, "looks like you're brushing and flossing pretty well. No cavities at all, but we'll have you come back next week for a cleaning. Make an appointment on your way out, all right?"

It was the first checkup I'd ever had when he didn't have to do *anything*. Was it the magic spell, or was it that Mom kept asking if I'd brushed and flossed, and only bought fruit instead of candy for snacks? I didn't know, but I was relieved.

And then came Friday.

Boy, was Friday something else.

10

M R S . Lowell had a reputation for being mean, but Friday she outdid herself.

Even people who never got in trouble with her didn't have a chance that day. Cindy Higgs got up to sharpen a pencil right after the papers had been passed out for a quiz, and Mrs. Lowell told her to take her seat at once.

Cindy looked startled. "But I need to sharpen this before I can do the quiz," she said.

"I told you, Cynthia, to take your seat." There was a pinched look around Mrs. Lowell's mouth.

"But I don't have a pencil!"

"You should have thought of that before class started."

"I did," Cindy told her. "It was sharp, then, but it just broke."

"Take your seat," the teacher said, and I thought her teeth were clenched. I caught Jeff's glance, and he rolled his eyes.

Bewildered and upset, Cindy dropped back into her seat. Bucky reached across and gave her one of his pencils, and she murmured her thanks. Even that was too much, apparently.

"You know the rules, Cynthia. There will be no talking once the quiz has been passed out. You may go to the office."

Cindy went bright red, and then so pale that her freckles stood out on her nose. "Mrs. Lowell, all I did was thank Bucky for the pencil—"

Mrs. Lowell slapped her ruler sharply on the desk, and Cindy's explanation trickled away. "I don't like to repeat myself," Mrs. Lowell said, and waited.

Crimson again, Cindy picked up her books and left the room. I thought she was trying not to cry. I couldn't remember Cindy ever being sent to the office before, and resentment rose inside me in a scalding wave. She shouldn't have been sent this time, either. My only consolation was that Mr. Hamilton was going to think this was a stupid reason to kick a kid out of class, and maybe he'd say so to Mrs. Lowell. Maybe he'd even fire her.

I knew the last part wasn't likely, but I hoped he bawled her out, so she'd know what it felt like.

In silence, we started the quiz. After a few minutes the only sound, other than the faint scratching of pencils on our papers, was Don Moore, snifling.

Mrs. Lowell's ruler hit her desk with a crack like a rifle shot, and we all jumped.

"Donald, don't you have a handkerchief?"

Don looked up, confused. "What?"

"Stop making that terrible noise," she told him.

"What noise?" He honestly didn't know what she was talking about, and I started to feel sorry for him.

This wasn't the right day to do or say anything stupid, but Don couldn't help it. He often didn't know what someone else was talking about unless they drew him a diagram.

"Blow your nose!" Mrs. Lowell exploded.

Now Don was embarrassed. "I ain't got a handkerchief."

"Then go in the restroom and use a paper towel!"

"Now?" he asked, more confused than ever.

"Now," she repeated, and he got up, looked around at Norm and Jim as if for help. He didn't get any, of course, so he shrugged and left the room. When he came back a few minutes later, he'd had sensed enough to bring a couple of extra paper towels with him, which indicated he was smarter than I'd thought.

The next person who got in trouble was Cal Solvang. The only time I could remember Cal getting sent to the office was last year when he tripped over a foot Norm stuck out in the aisle in front of him, and they'd exchanged a few punches. Mr. Hamilton just shook his head that time and sent him to study hall for the rest of the period until the teacher cooled off.

Cal had trouble with warts. He'd tried everything to get rid of them. They'd been burned off and cut off and frozen off and they kept growing back.

The first I knew there was any problem was when Cal suddenly stood up—he sat about halfway toward the front of the room from me—in the middle of what Mrs. Lowell was saying about the next day's assignment.

"Where do you think you're going?" she demanded.

Cal held up a hand, and we could see the blood running off his knuckles into his sleeve. "I knocked off a wart. I thought I'd better go get it stopped bleeding."

Instead of telling him to go ahead and attend to it, she pressed her lips together for a moment before she spoke. She reminded me that Halloween wasn't far away; she could pass as a witch even without a costume, I thought.

"How did you manage this, if you were paying attention to what you were supposed to be doing?"

Cal's back was to me, and I saw his ears getting red. "I guess I wasn't thinking about it, and I chewed on it."

This time it was Mrs. Lowell who began to turn red. She sort of swelled up, too, like a toad can do when it doesn't want to be swallowed by a snake. "Get out," she said in a deadly voice. "Get out of my classroom and don't come back!"

Cal didn't say any more. Neither did anyone else, though we looked at each other. Did she mean he wasn't to come back, *ever?* Five minutes later, while Mrs. Lowell was in the middle of writing on the blackboard so hard she kept snapping the chalk, the fire alarm rang.

We had fire drills regularly, and everybody considered them an excuse to get out of class for a few minutes. Only this time, when we filed out into the hallway, we smelled smoke.

"Hey! There's really a fire!" somebody yelled, and the next thing I knew there were kids squealing and a few of them pushing. Most of us did what we were supposed to do, filing out in an orderly way, but not everybody stayed cool. Just as Mrs. Lowell followed the last of our class into the corridor, a couple of scared kids started to run and knocked her flat.

Jeff was right behind me, and when I stopped, he ran into me. The smell of smoke was stronger already, although we couldn't see it or any flames, and while I didn't feel panic, I wanted to get outside as quickly as possible. But the teacher was sprawled there looking dazed; her head had struck the doorframe, and I wasn't sure she was going to get up.

I looked around and didn't see any other teachers close enough to help; they were all getting their classes out of the building quickly.

"Mrs. Lowell?" I said uncertainly. She didn't reply. In fact her eyes had gone half-shut.

I muttered a curse under my breath.

"Maybe we better see if we can get her on her feet," Jeff said, and he sounded as uncomfortable as I felt. We didn't really want to touch her, but she wasn't getting up, and we didn't know what else to do.

"You get one arm and I'll get the other one," Jeff said. "Maybe she can walk if we get her up."

So we did. She wasn't as heavy as we expected, and she managed to stagger along between us until we got her outside. Kids were milling around on the lawn. Usually the teachers kept them in lines until the bell sounded for us to go back inside; but this time they knew there was really something wrong, and they'd grouped together to talk. They called out to Mr. Fitch, the head janitor, and he was waving his arms around, explaining what had happened. I caught something about an explosion in the boiler room.

We stood there for a minute, propping up Mrs. Lowell between us. "Are you all right?" Jeff asked her, and she didn't answer.

"What do we do now?" I asked. She suddenly sagged at the knees, and my question was answered because we didn't have any choice except to lower her to the ground.

Mr. Jaeger, the art teacher, saw us and came over at once. "What's happened here?" He knelt and checked her pulse, and we explained how she'd gotten knocked down. Just then we heard sirens, and Mr. Jaeger turned to Mr. Hamilton, who was coming out of the front doors, probably the last one to leave the building.

"I think we need an ambulance here, George," Mr. Jaeger called. "She may have a concussion from being knocked down, or she may have had a heart attack. Can we get at a phone to call?"

"The fire department'll be able to call for an aide car," Mr. Hamilton decided, turning as the big trucks came roaring up.

Jeff and I felt better when the teachers had taken over. We moved off to where Bucky and some other kids were standing. Smoke was coming from the back of the school; one of the fire trucks was on the lawn, and another was cutting across the playground. Two more pulled up in front, and men jumped out and ran inside, pulling hoses after them.

The aide car came, siren screaming, and the Emergency Medical Technicians jumped out and ran to Mrs. Lowell. One of them took her blood pressure and her pulse, and a minute later she was lifted onto a stretcher and carried away. They used the siren then, too. I figured it was fairly serious.

It would have been sort of fun watching all the activity around the school if I hadn't been wondering if we'd caused any of this with our spells.

I wasn't the only one who wondered about it. Bucky's eyes were wide as the three of us stepped apart from the others, where we could talk without being overheard. "Jeez," he said, watching the firemen swarming over the place. By now a tanker truck had arrived and was heading for the back of the school, too. "This wasn't exactly what I had in mind when Jeff suggested making the school close today."

"Noooo," Jeff said slowly. "Maybe they won't close the school, though."

"But I hit a home run, even if it did break a window, and Alex had a good dental checkup—and we're out of school for now."

"I don't see how Mrs. Lowell is going to learn any lesson from this," I contributed. "What if she's really hurt, or had a heart attack or something else serious?"

"We couldn't have done that with our spell," Jeff said, sounding as uneasy as I felt. "I mean, we didn't dream up a fire, did we? Or those kids who ran into her?"

Somehow it was impossible to feel completely confident that we had no responsibility in any of this. I was remembering that part in the front of the magic book that warned amateurs against undertaking the spells too lightly, because the consequences could be serious. What had it said? "The reader should soberly consider the potential results, some of which may be irrevocable." I didn't quote that out loud, but I could tell by Bucky's face that he was remembering too, even if Jeff still thought it was all a coincidence.

"We weren't trying to do anything really terrible to anybody," he said.

A few minutes later, Mr. Hamilton climbed up on one of the trucks standing on the grass and waved his arms to get our attention. "Students! Quiet down, please! I have an announcement."

Voices subsided, and all faces turned toward the principal.

"We have had an explosion in the boiler room, and there's a fire. It probably won't cause a great deal of damage, not enough to close school for long, but because the firemen will be working here for several hours, we are closing for the rest of the day. You may all go home. If you need to contact your parents at work, you may come to the front door and we'll take you inside a few at a time to call. I'll expect to see all of you here as usual on Monday morning."

There were a few cheers and whistles, and some of the kids broke away from the groups on the lawn and headed for home. More of them hung around, hoping there'd be something interesting to see.

There wasn't, though. The smoke was diminishing and all the activity was inside, out of our sight. After about twenty minutes, two of the trucks headed back to the station, and the firemen from the other ones were busy inside.

"Come on, let's go," Bucky said finally. "We wanted a day off, so let's do something with it."

He didn't suggest doing another spell, though, and neither did Jeff or I. We'd all left our lunches in our lockers, and they didn't want us to go and get them, so we had to go home for lunch.

"Come on over after you eat, and we'll think of something to do," I said. "No use wasting a perfectly good day off."

That didn't work out, though. Jeff called while I was fixing tacos for myself.

"My mom says since I don't have school, I have to

clean my room today instead of waiting until Saturday."

I was silent for a moment. Then I said, "I guess you won't have to wreck Saturday morning doing it, then."

He sounded funny, too. "I was thinking more in terms of just coming home and finding it done. Not having to do it myself a day early."

"It's crazy," I said. "But, in a way, all the spells worked. None of them quite the way we thought."

"Yeah. Well, see you tomorrow, Alex," he said, and hung up.

"What was all that about?" Mike wanted to know. "What spells are you talking about?"

"Oh, just a joke," I told him. But after he'd gone over to Paul's, I sat there at the kitchen table for a while, thinking.

What if we really had made all those things happen? What if we'd killed Mrs. Lowell?

When I went upstairs a few minutes later, the magic book was lying on my nightstand. I didn't touch it. I didn't even want to look at it. It sent shivers down my spine just to see it there, looking old and worn and innocent, when I didn't think it was innocent at all.

What had I gotten myself into when I brought that book home?

11

WHEN the paper came, I ran out and got it and looked for a story on the fire at school. I guess the paper must already have gone to press when the fire happened, though, because there wasn't anything about it, or about Mrs. Lowell.

It wasn't until the six o'clock news that I heard anything, and then it wasn't what I was worried about. I already knew the school hadn't burned down.

They showed a picture of our school with the smoke rising, and the fire trucks and the aide car driving away, but the announcer didn't say anything about a teacher collapsing and having to be taken to the hospital.

It couldn't have been our spell, I kept telling myself, that made her get knocked down and hurt. The spell had been to teach her a lesson, and what could that teach her? Yet I felt more and more guilty.

It was weird. All I'd really wanted from that fool book was a spell to make Norm leave me alone, and I hadn't been able to do that one because it disappeared.

We'd only tried most of the other things for the fun of it.

Only it wasn't being that much fun.

On impulse, I ran upstairs and picked up the magic book and ran downstairs with it. I'd get rid of it, once and for all, I thought. It had promised me a spell to use against Norm, when I first saw it, and then it had taken the spell away, so the heck with it. I tried not to think what Jeff and Bucky would say when I told them what I'd done.

I carried the book outside and dropped it into the garbage can. Strangely enough, though, I didn't feel any better.

We were sitting down to dinner when the telephone rang.

Dad frowned. He gets a lot of emergency calls during mealtimes, and he won't let the rest of us take calls then. Not even Deidra is allowed to answer her phone during dinner.

"Graden residence," he said into the receiver. Sometimes he forgets and says, "Supreme Trucking."

His expression changed then, and I was really startled when he handed the phone to me. "It's for you, Alex. It's the school principal."

I felt as if he'd handed me a snake. What kind of bad news was I going to get? He couldn't know my spell had caused a fire in the school, or . . . "Yes, hello," I said, and my voice squeaked.

"Alex, I just wanted to commend you for your performance this morning."

Confused, I didn't know what to say. What performance?

84

"It was quick thinking for you and Jeff Saul to get Mrs. Lowell out of the building the way you did."

"But—there wasn't really a fire," I said stupidly. "I mean, she wasn't in any danger."

"Only of being trampled further, maybe," he said. "Although at the time you certainly couldn't have known that. I've just visited her in the hospital, and she remembers being knocked down, and you and Jeff helping her. She asked me to express her gratitude."

"Uh—well, she's going to be all right, then?"

"She sustained a concussion in the fall," Mr. Hamilton said. "That isn't going to cause any long-range problems, though, and in a way it was a lucky accident. She's been feeling unwell for some time, and her daughter hadn't been able to get her to see a doctor. Once she got to the hospital, however, they did a lot of routine tests and discovered that she has several serious medical problems, diabetes and high blood pressure. Fortunately, both of these are treatable, and she'll be getting the care she needs. It's quite possible that being taken to the hospital today saved her life."

"But I didn't know—" I broke off uncertainly. "You mean she's had these things wrong with her for a long time?"

"Apparently so. Of course, I don't expect you to discuss this outside your own family, Alex, but she wanted you to know how appreciative she is that you helped her. And with treatment she'll undoubtedly be feeling much better. She had actually been wondering if she could get through another school year, or if she should retire. Now it's likely she'll continue to teach until regular retirement age."

When I hung up, I was more confused than ever. If she'd had health problems for months before I even found the magic book, how could I have had anything to do with what was wrong with her? I mean, getting knocked down might have saved her life, and maybe taught her she ought to see a doctor when she was sick, but it couldn't have taught her any lesson about being disagreeable in class, could it?

Mr. Hamilton's words kept filtering through my head as I slid into my chair. What would Jeff think about our actions making Mrs. Lowell decide to keep on teaching instead of retiring? The kids would like nothing better than to see her retire.

Then I was struck by another thought. Was the fact that she was sick the reason Mrs. Lowell had been short-tempered and unfair? I remembered how cranky Dad was the couple of weeks he was laid up at home with broken ribs after he had an accident with a truck. Mom told us to be careful not to bother him, because he was hurting and restless because he couldn't go to work, and that was why he was irritable. The more I thought about it, the more confused I got. I didn't have any way of knowing what would have happened if I hadn't worked any of the spells. Maybe I shouldn't have thrown the book away after all.

After dinner I went outside and took the lid off the garbage can.

There were potato peelings and oninon peelings and grapefruit rinds, but no book. I poked around almost to the bottom of the can, but it wasn't there.

I didn't know if I was sorry or glad when I walked back into the house without it.

JEFF looked at me in disbelief. "You're crazy, Alex! How could you throw it away?"

I shrugged, jamming my hands in my pockets. "I thought it was getting us into trouble."

"The garbage hasn't been picked up," Jeff said. "Not until Tuesday. So what happened to the book?"

"Maybe it magicked itself somewhere else," I suggested. "Or someone came along checking through garbage cans and took it."

Jeff shook his head. "I can't believe you'd pitch it out. We never even took care of Norm!"

"Yeah, I know. I was beginning to think we wouldn't dare try, anyway. I mean, none of the spells exactly turned out the way we expected."

"That's probably because we're beginners, and we didn't do everything right. It could be partly my fault. I mean, maybe if we'd used real holly berries instead of artificial ones, it might have made a difference. The spell might have turned out different."

"It doesn't matter now, I guess," I said. "The book's gone."

But that night, when I came out of the bathroom to go to bed, thre was a familiar worn blue-black book lying on my nightstand.

I stopped in the middle of the room, almost forgetting to breathe.

Mike was already in bed, propped up reading a book on drawing wildlife.

"Mike," I said. My voice sounded as if I'd been running.

"What?" He didn't look away from his book.

"Did you—put that book on my nightstand?"

He gave me an annoyed glance. "I haven't touched anything of yours, Alex. Why are you always bugging me?"

"I didn't mean to bug you. But that book wasn't there when I went downstairs for supper."

"Well, I never moved it." He reached up and turned off his light, then rolled over with his back to me. "Good night."

"Good night," I echoed. I got into bed, knowing I wasn't going to go right to sleep. I adjusted my own light so it wouldn't shine in Mike's face if he rolled toward me and picked up the book. It was very heavy against my raised legs.

How had it gotten back into the house? In my imagination I could see it pushing at the lid on the garbage can, slithering out through the opening that made, and then struggling across the yard, prying open the screen door, and bumping and thumping its way up the stairs to my room. Or maybe it had floated through the air, since nobody had heard it. I was convinced it had returned of its own accord. It raised prickles on the back of my neck and sent that tingling sensation through my fingers at the same time.

I opened it and started to turn the pages, and there it was.

The spell that we'd been unable to find since the first day we looked at the book, the one to put an end to a bully's ways.

My heart hammered, and I began to read.

12

I COULDN'T wait to tell Jeff. My fingers were shaking as I copied out the spell into a notebook; I wasn't taking a chance on losing it again.

I thought about calling him, but I knew his folks wouldn't like it, since it was after ten o'clock and we were both supposed to be asleep. Only I didn't think I could go to sleep without telling someone.

After a few minutes of lying there rigid with tension, I got up and pulled on my jeans and a T-shirt, then reached for a sweatshirt and my Nikes. With those in hand I crept downstairs.

I heard my mom and dad talking in their bedroom, and there was a line of light under the door. The rest of the house was dark, though the streetlights filtered through the curtains enough so I could find my way out the back door.

I sat down on the steps and put on the shoes, then shrugged into the sweatshirt. I didn't know if it was really chilly enough for it or if I was just having goose bumps with excitement.

Jeff only lives a block away. It's less than that if you cut through the alley, which I did. Though there were lights in the living room windows, I knew Jeff wouldn't be there this time of night. I walked around the side of the house and groped in the driveway for some gravel, hoping I could hit the right window.

I threw one rock at a time. Even so, it made quite a bit of noise in the night stillness. It took three before the window suddenly shot open and Jeff stuck his head out. "Who is it? What's going on?"

"It's me, Alex. I found the spell for a bully," I hissed.

"No kidding?" He leaned farther out and spoke more loudly.

"What do we have to get?" He sounded as excited as I felt.

"The fur from a brown rabbit," I recited. "A toadstool. The tooth of a four-footed animal, it doesn't specify any particular one. And—" for a moment my throat closed, and then I said the words, "moss from a tombstone, gathered at midnight."

Jeff's whistle floated down to me. "Boy, that's quite an assortment. My uncle has rabbits, but I think they're all either white or white and black. Somebody must have brown ones, though, or are those all wild?"

"I don't know anything about rabbits. I think there are some brown ones at the petting zoo in Everett, though. Do you think we can get toadstools this time of year?"

"Is a mushroom a toadstool? The supermarket has mushrooms all the time."

"It says toadstool. I think we'd better be careful to

use exactly what the spell calls for. We don't want anything freaky to happen because we didn't do it exactly
right."

"Moss off a tombstone, gathered at midnight. It
gives me shivers," Jeff said, but he sounded wound up,
too, the same as I was. "How'd you find the spell again,
Alex?"

"I don't know. I threw the book out, and somehow
it got back into my room, and I started reading it again,
and there it was." I hesitated, wondering if I'd sound like
a fool, then said what I thought, anyway. What good
was a friend if you couldn't express a stupid idea to him
once in a while? "It's almost as if the book showed us
that special spell about the bully to get us intrigued in
the first place. And then it took the spell away until we
learned something first. Responsibility, maybe? Or just
how to do smaller spells before we work up to the bigger
ones? And now it's put the bully spell back in because
we're ready to do it. Jeff, I think it *wants* us to teach
Norm a lesson."

Jeff didn't jeer at me. "Well, he sure needs one. You
tell Bucky yet?"

"No. I'll tell him tomorrow. I couldn't wait until
morning without telling someone, though."

"I won't be able to sleep," Jeff said, laughing a little.

"I won't, either," I told him. "I'll see you tomorrow."

I did sleep, though, and I had a wild dream about
Norm chasing me with a sword. I kept hearing it swish-
ing through the air on both sides of me, close to my ears,
and I ran and ran until I was out of breath. And then I
tripped over a rock and went sprawling. When I rolled
over and looked up, Norm was standing over me, grin-

ning, waiting to slice that wicked blade across my throat.

I woke up, gasping, fighting him off with my hands flailing around.

Mike was staring down at me, his eyes unfocused without his glasses. "Hey, Alex! Wake up!"

I fell back on the pillow, breathing heavily. "Sorry I woke you up. I was having a nightmare," I told him.

It was still dark, but I didn't go back to sleep right away. I lay there thinking about the spell we were going to work as soon as we got the right ingredients, hoping I'd be able to give Norm as interesting a nightmare as he'd given me.

W E had a substitute teacher on Monday. Her name was Miss Miles and she was young and pretty, with curly blonde hair. She told us that Mrs. Lowell was out of the hospital and would be recuperating at home for the week, and in the meantime she hoped we'd all get along well with *her*. As usual when we have a sub, the kids tried to put various things over on her. Norm told her we had open book tests in math, and she only smiled and said, "Well, not in my classes, so put the book away, please." Cindy Higgs told her that we often moved the class out onto the lawn on nice days, and Miss Miles said, "I think we'll manage better inside. We can open the windows to take advantage of the weather, though."

No matter what anyone said, Miss Miles kept on smiling and ignored all our suggestions. Jim Moore wasn't the only kid who hung around her desk after class, asking for extra help with math. Even Norm did, and he didn't need help any more than I did.

We'd told Bucky the things we needed to do the spell on Norm, and I copied the list to give one to him and one to Jeff, so we could all try to get them. We'd already agreed that when we got everything else, we'd go together to the graveyard at midnight for the moss. There was nothing in the book that said it had to be gathered by one person.

We decided to go together to try for the rabbit fur, too. Bucky had a neighbor who had a brown rabbit in a hutch behind their house, and he thought we could get at it without being seen because the people both worked until after five.

We took some scissors, since we didn't know how difficult it would be to pull hair out. Rabbits, Bucky informed us, could make more noise than you'd think if they were hurt or frightened.

We went after school on Monday. I had a small plastic bag in my pocket to hold the fur, and Bucky had scissors. We went down the alley and approached the house from the rear.

It was fine until we actually approached the rabbit cages. We could see them—four white rabbits and a brown one—and we walked right into the yard from the alley. There were no cars in the driveway or the carport, so it seemed safe enough. There was a fence and a gate, which wasn't locked.

We were halfway to the hutches when this dog came hurtling around the corner of the house, barking furiously.

We came to a stop, facing a monster of an animal showing his fangs and acting as if he'd eat the three of us for a snack, sort of a cross between a Great Dane and a pit bull. He was about the size of the ponies they have for kids to ride at the Seattle zoo. I gulped and dove over the fence, figuring I didn't have time to open the gate, get through it, and close it behind me before that dog reached me.

I went over more or less head first and landed in a clatter on the garbage cans in the alley. Jeff was right behind me, but though he missed the garbage cans, he caught his pants on a nail in the fence. I heard him yelp, then start cursing under his breath.

The dog hit the fence right behind us, in a frenzy now, leaping up and biting the air where we'd just been. I got up and turned toward Jeff, hoping the dog couldn't leap over after us; his teeth reminded me of a saber-toothed tiger I'd once seen in a movie.

"My mom's going to kill me," Jeff moaned, looking at the three-cornered tear in his new jeans.

"That dog would have killed you if you hadn't made it over the fence," I said. "How come Bucky didn't know about the dog? Where is Bucky, anyway?"

Jeff was distracted from his torn jeans. "Bucky? Where are you?"

The dog was still leaping at the fence, thudding against it with a sickening sound, barking like a maniac. We couldn't see Bucky.

"He didn't get eaten, did he?" Jeff moved away from the dog, checked to make sure the gate was securely closed, then yelled again. "Bucky! Where are you?"

The voice was unsteady. "I'm up here. Hey, guys, how am I going to get out of this yard?"

I tipped my head and saw him, then. He'd figured he was too far from the gate and too awkward to get over the fence in one bound the way Jeff and I had, so he'd shinnied up a maple tree.

He was clinging to it now, his round face showing

every freckle. "They must've just got the dog," he said. "They never had one before."

Jeff stared at him. "How you going to get out of there, Bucky?"

"Now, wait a darn minute. You guys got me into this, you gotta help me get out!" Bucky protested. His foot slipped on the branch it was resting on, and for a moment he dangled by his arms from a higher branch. "You gotta find a way to get that dog away from me!"

"How?" Jeff asked reasonably. "You're the one who lives a couple of houses down; you should have known about the dog."

"What is there we can do?" I asked. "If we open that gate, the dog'll take off after us, and I'm pretty sure he can run faster than we can. We can't let him out, Bucky. He might get hit by a car or something."

Bucky tried to move up one limb on the tree, because the dog had discovered where he was. He had left the fence and was growling and leaping up trying to reach Bucky's feet.

"Come on, guys! Think of something!" Bucky pleaded.

"A spell," Jeff said suddenly. "We could put a spell on him, make him quiet down so you could get out of the yard."

"The book's at home," I protested. "I'd have to go get it, and look up a likely spell, get the stuff to make it, and I don't know if Bucky can hang on that long."

The dog leaped again, and his fangs raked the side of Bucky's tennis shoe. Bucky howled, and this time he made it up one more limb of the maple. He was beyond reach of the dog, now.

"Do it!" he cried. "Get the book, do a spell! Get me

out of here before the Falkners come home and find me here and call the police!"

"What if the spell calls for something we can't find?" Jeff asked.

Bucky looked near to tears. "Please, Alex! Hurry!"

"You'd better come with me," I told Jeff. "In case it takes two of us to gather what we need."

We left Bucky hanging in the tree, and the dog guarding the foot of it; we ran through the alley as if we were trying to make points at a track meet.

"I hope there is such a spell," Jeff panted as we ran. "What'll we do if we can't find one that seems appropriate?"

I was too busy running to answer. Besides, I didn't want to think about such a possibility.

If we couldn't get Bucky out of that tree and the yard, we'd all be in trouble.

13

J E F F and I ran all the way to my house. We were puffing when we got there, and I brought out the magic book and opened it on the table.

"What do we look for?" I panted. "This is crazy, Jeff. If we need strange ingredients for a spell, it may take hours, or days, to get them. The Falkners will come home and hear their dog and call the police before we can do anything."

"Outside of drugging the dog, what else can we do? We don't have any sleeping pills at our house, and even if we did, I think they'd take too long to work in this case." Jeff was leafing through the pages, skimming the titles to the spells.

"We don't have anything like that, either. And we can't poison the dog, not even to rescue Bucky. How are we are going to explain why we were in the Falkners' yard?"

"Wait!" Jeff had been running a finger down a page and he stopped. "Don't give up yet. How about this? *Spell to bring on a deep sleep*. Wouldn't that do it? If we could make the dog fall asleep? It would only have to be for a few minutes, long enough for Bucky to slide out of the tree and make it through the gate."

"Sounds good," I agreed, then asked nervously, "What do we need to work the spell?"

"That's the best part. Listen to this: oil of cloves—Mom keeps some in the emergency medical chest in case one of us gets a toothache while we're camping or traveling—some cedar shavings, which I can get off the tree in the front yard, poppy seeds—"

"Mom keeps those in her spice jars," I interrupted.

"—And two small white stones."

"White?" I echoed. "Are there any white ones in your driveway? I remember mostly gray ones."

"Get the poppy seeds, and we'll go see," Jeff said. "You think we'd better take the book with us, in case it doesn't work and we have to look for something else?"

"If this one doesn't work, we aren't going to have time for a second spell," I said dismally. "But bring it, I guess."

It was nearly five o'clock when we trotted up the alley to the Falkners' back gate. We didn't hear the dog, and for a minute I hoped maybe he'd given up and gone away.

But there was Bucky, still clinging to a limb, and when we reached the fence, the dog rose and growled at us from the position he'd taken guarding the bottom of the tree.

"It took you long enough," Bucky said. "Hurry up, my arm's getting numb from hanging onto this branch over my head."

"We've got a spell," Jeff told him, holding up the cup we were carrying the ingredients in. "Just hang on a little longer, and we'll put the dog to sleep. Then be ready to come down and run for the gate."

"How you going to get that stuff on him?" Bucky wanted to know.

"It doesn't say we have to get it on him. We have to stir it up and then read some words. I'll stir, Alex, and you read."

We rested the magic book on the lid of a garbage can, and while Jeff stirred with a stick—we'd learned our lesson about stirring with a finger—I read out the strange words. I didn't know what they meant—they didn't sound like anything I'd ever heard before—but they gave me goose bumps.

We waited.

Jeff put down the cup with the potion in it and prepared to open the gate the minute Bucky started down the tree.

The dog must have been somewhat tired already, because he'd stopped barking, though whenever we looked directly at him, he drew back his lips in a snarl. But he still stayed close to the bottom of the tree, right under Bucky's feet, which were just out of reach above him.

We waited some more.

"I don't think it's going to work," I said uneasily. "He's just sitting there, the same as he was. Maybe these spells don't work on animals, only on people."

"It'll probably take awhile," Jeff said, but he sounded uncertain, too. "Go to sleep, doggy. Go to sleep."

The dog looked him in the eye and growled, low in his massive throat.

After a few minutes, Jeff looked at me. "You're right. It isn't working. What do we do now?"

It was at that moment that Bucky suddenly released his hold on the branch over his head and his feet slipped off the branch he'd been standing on.

He landed right on the dog, which gave a surprised "Woof" and backed out of the way.

Bucky lay there in a heap, and the dog that had been so menacing for the past hour stood a few feet away, staring at him in astonishment.

"Come on, hurry up!" Jeff yelled, unlatching the gate, ready to open it the minute Bucky got close to it. But Bucky didn't move, and after a few seconds I realized why.

"He's asleep!" I yelled. "The spell didn't work on the dog, it worked on Bucky! He's sound asleep!"

Jeff leaned against the fence. His mouth sagged open. "Oh, no! Bucky, wake up! Get up before he kills you!"

Actually, the dog wasn't doing anything except standing there. I think he was as bewildered as everybody else.

"Bucky!" I yelled. "Wake up! Get up, hurry!" The Falkners might show up any minute, and it wouldn't be any easier to explain Bucky asleep in the middle of their backyard than it would have been to explain him up their maple tree.

The dog took a cautious step toward the fallen Bucky, and Jeff and I both yelled again. The dog looked at us, then lowered his head toward Bucky's.

He didn't bite, though. He wasn't growling any longer. He put out a pink tongue and tentatively licked Bucky's cheek.

Bucky stirred, raising a hand to fend off the tongue, and opened his eyes.

He told us later he'd been convinced he was going to be eaten alive right at that moment. We saw his eyes flare wide open, and he made a choking sound. "N-n-no! Nooo!"

"Get up," I urged. "Come on, he doesn't know what's happening. He isn't going to bite if you hurry up and get out of there!"

For a few seconds it seemed that Bucky was paralyzed. Then he rolled over, away from the beast inspecting him, and scrambled to his feet. Jeff almost forgot to open the gate fast enough, but the dog wasn't even chasing Bucky. He sank onto his haunches and looked at us with his tongue hanging out.

Bucky collapsed against the garbage cans and tried to get his breath after Jeff slammed the gate shut and latched it. "I thought I was going to die there before you guys got back."

"Sorry it took so long," I apologized. "But you're safe now. Only we still don't have the brown rabbit's fur."

Bucky looked over the fence at the dog and shuddered. "We'll have to get it somewhere else, unless you guys want to go in there and get it. I'm *never* going back in that yard."

Jeff and I decided we wouldn't, either. Maybe the dog had gotten used to us and wouldn't do anything, now, but nobody wanted to chance it.

We'd have to wait until Saturday and take the bus to Everett and visit the petting zoo. Maybe there'd be a chance to get some fur there.

The other ingredients for the potion weren't much easier to get. We couldn't find any toadstools and none of the four-legged animals of our acquaintance showed any inclination to part with their teeth, short of our pulling them.

Jeff finally had an idea about that one. "You know Dr. Waters, the veterinarian? Sometimes he pulls teeth. It could be from a dog or a cat or a cow or a horse or anything else with four feet, right?"

"You ask him," I said. "Why are you going to say you want it, in case he's saved any?"

"I'll say it's for a school project. In a way that's the truth, isn't it? A project to get Norm to stop ruining every day we go to school."

Dr. Waters accepted his explanation of why he wanted a tooth, but he didn't have one. He said he'd let Jeff know if he acquired one in the near future. He couldn't promise anything. He wasn't often called upon to do extractions.

We kept talking about the moss from a tombstone, but since we couldn't use it until we had the other stuff anyway, we didn't see any rush about that.

"Maybe it would be a good idea to make sure there is some, though," Jeff said. "Let's go over to the cemetery on Eightieth Street and see."

We went there after school, and it was a big disappointment. It's a good sized cemetery and there were plenty of graves; but most of them were marked with little flat stone slabs set flush with the ground, and they didn't have any moss on them.

"There's another graveyard over behind St. Andrew's," Jeff said as we walked toward home. "It's a lot older than this one, and maybe nobody keeps the moss from growing there. Let's try it."

None of us belonged to St. Andrew's. We weren't sure how the priest would take it if he caught us there.

The gate was open, though, and there was no sign saying to keep out.

It was a warm, sunny afternoon, and there were red and yellow leaves all over the ground, not like the other cemetery where the grass was freshly mowed and the leaves had all been raked up.

A lot of the headstones were very old. We stopped and read some of them, about people who had died as much as a hundred years ago. The oldest stones in the whole place were in the very back, the farthest row from the gate, and there we finally struck pay dirt. Some of the tombstones were black with mildew. You had to scrape it off with a stick to read the words chiseled underneath. And a few had green moss growing like a regular carpet over them.

"This is it," Bucky said cheerfully. "This is where we'll come when it's time to get the moss."

"At midnight," Jeff said in a hollow voice. "I wonder if there are ghosts walking here at midnight?"

Bucky stopped smiling. "Cut it out. Come on, let's go home. I'm hungry." I had to admit that even I felt better once we left the cemetery.

The following evening the veterinarian called to tell Jeff he had a tooth from a horse for him. We had the first item of the four we needed.

The day after that, Bucky went to the variety store for his mother and came back with a rabbit's foot made into a key ring, which he displayed triumphantly.

"You sure it's a real one?" I demanded. "We've had some peculiar results with these spells, and from now on we'd better stick to the literal requirements. We don't want to take any chances with this one; it's the most important of all."

"It's real. See, it says *genuine rabbit's foot*." He dropped it into my hand.

"OK. So now we need a toadstool, and then we can go after the moss."

Several times we each got yelled at for stepping into someone's yard to look around the bases of trees for toadstools. My mom said they sometimes grew around alder trees, and there were plenty of those, but I was beginning to think it was the wrong time of year. We were having so much trouble trying to find a toadstool that we'd have given up, I think, if it hadn't been for Norm.

He pretended to accidentally push my clothes into the shower after P.E., so I had to go back to class with a wet shirt and socks. He knocked Jeff's notebook out of his hands and then stepped on the papers in muddy shoes and Jeff had to copy his English paper over before he could turn it in.

On Friday Jeff and I approached school and saw Norm and Jim and Don standing in Mrs. Halliday's yard, stomping on something and laughing. We paused, waiting for Bucky to catch up with us, hoping they'd have gone on before we got there.

"Probably killing her cat," Jeff muttered. "They wouldn't be having so much fun at whatever they're doing if it wasn't mean."

When we got there, however, after Norm and his buddies had taken off across the street to torment a couple of little kids by taking their lunch sacks and throwing them up into a tree, it wasn't a cat that was smashed on the ground.

It was a whole patch of toadstools.

Jeff looked at them in disgust. "There isn't a whole

one left. You suppose we have to have a whole one, or can we use one that's mangled?"

"I'd feel safer with a whole one," I said. "Let's see if there are any more on the other side of that tree."

And there they were. A whole batch of little tiny brown toadstools. I picked half a dozen of them, thinking I'd put the extras in the freezer for future use, and we went on across the street, too. The two little kids were crying about their lunches, so Jeff climbed on my back and reached up to get them.

"One thing for sure," he said, as the little kids accepted the lunch bags, "we've got to carry through on this. Somebody's got to stop Norm."

So we agreed to meet and go to the graveyard at midnight that night.

It gave me prickles down my spine, just thinking of it, but I knew Jeff was right. Whatever it took to stop Norm, we had to do it.

14

IT WAS a strange thing. During that week Jim got at least C's, and a couple of B's, not only on his math papers but on some of the other ones, too. Besides that miracle, his cousin got C's, too.

After Don's second passing grade in math, which Bucky noticed as he handed back the papers, Bucky got curious enough to ask. "How you doing it?"

Don looked embarrassed yet pleased with himself. "I been doing my homework with Jim," he said. "Jim understands how to do it now."

So without our working any more spells on either of them, they were both upgrading their school work. We didn't know if we should take the credit or not, for having gotten Jim his first good mark.

"Maybe it felt good not to be at the bottom of the class for once," Jeff said thoughtfully, "so he decided to try working for a while."

One effect this had was that the Moores didn't seem to be hanging around after school with Norm quite so much. Jeff and I came out one afternoon and saw Norm trying to start something with Hugh Doyle, blocking his way so Hugh had to step off the sidewalk. Only Norm decided not to let him go around, either.

"Get out of the way," Hugh said, starting to look tense.

"You going to make us?" Norm taunted. "We're going to keep you here until we're ready to let you go, right, guys?"

Don and Jim looked at each other and shuffled their feet. "Well, uh, we got a lot of homework tonight," Jim said. "We have to go, Norm. My dad said if I got at least C on the test next week, he'd take me to a Mariner's game."

"Me, too," Don echoed. "I mean, my dad said he would, too."

The minute they turned away from Norm's astonished face, Hugh lunged through the opening Don and Jim had left and trotted toward the street. It was the first time any of us could remember that the Moores hadn't backed up Norm, and it was clearly disconcerting to him.

"He likes it better when it's three to one in his own favor," Jeff observed as we followed after Hugh. "Tomorrow night we're going to go get the moss, right?"

"Right," I agreed.

Only before we got around to that, there was another nasty episode with Norm. It only proved how important it was for us to turn the tables on him.

On Friday afternoon Bucky stayed late to talk to Miss Miles about a quiz he hadn't done very well on, and Jeff's mother picked *him* up because they had to go see his grandmother. She'd fallen down the steps at her house, and though she hadn't broken any bones, she was badly shaken and upset.

Jeff promised he'd meet me later, as we'd planned, so we could gather the moss from the tombstone. I found myself hoping nothing would keep him at his grandmother's overnight. There would still be Bucky to go with me, but I thought I'd feel safer with three of us.

Anyway, that's why I was walking home alone, which I didn't often do. So there was only me when I encountered Norm Winthrop.

I recognized his red sweater ahead of me, and I was in the process of deciding to take a longer way home to avoid him when I realized that the younger kid he was talking to was my little brother Mike.

Mike was kneeling beside something on the sidewalk, and Norm had taken his usual menacing stance beside him. Just as Mike reached for what looked like a dead bird, Norm kicked the object out of his reach. The trouble was, he also managed to knock off Mike's glasses. I saw them go skidding off the curb into the street.

For a minute my throat closed up and I couldn't breathe. Then I moved toward him without thinking any further. All I knew was I couldn't let him hurt Mike again.

Norm heard me coming and turned around, and I could tell from his face that he wasn't worried about me being able to stop him. "Well, hi, Alexander."

I swallowed around the lump in my throat. "I think you better leave Mike alone."

"Oh? Who's gonna make me?"

Mike slowly rose and reached for his glasses. When he put them on, I saw that though they weren't broken, the frame was sprung, so they didn't sit right on his nose; one side was higher than the other.

I hadn't answered Norm yet, and he kicked out again at the bird—a robin—before Mike could pick it up.

"You think you can make me leave him alone?" Norm taunted.

I don't know where the words—or the courage to speak them—came from. I only knew I had to say them. "You touch him again, and I'll break your nose," I said, and realized my hands were doubled up into fists.

Uncertainty flickered in Norm's eyes. "You do, and I'll leave you lying here unconscious, Alex."

He was not much bigger than I was, and only a little heavier, but I knew he could lick me. We'd wrestled in P.E., and I'd never beaten him, though once or twice it was a tie. Again the words came without any conscious thought on my part.

"Maybe so, Norm," I said. "But you'll still have a broken nose of your own."

The uncertainty grew. He didn't have Don and Jim to back him up this time; it would be one on one, even if he did know he could lick me.

There was no one else around, and I was a block from home. If he pushed it, I was probably going to get beat up. My heart was pounding so hard I felt deafened by it, and I could feel the sweat breaking out all over me. Yet I couldn't let him hurt Mike because he had it in for me.

My little brother wiggled his glasses, trying to get them into a position where he could see through the right part. He always looked sober, so I couldn't tell if he was as scared as I was or not.

The silence stretched, and then I bent over, picked up the dead bird and put a hand on Mike's shoulder. "Come on, let's go home, " I told him.

Norm didn't move, so we stepped around him. I kept expecting him to hit me from behind. But I wouldn't give him the satisfaction of turning around to see what he was doing.

The rock hit me between the shoulder blades, and though I'd been anticipating something like that, it was a shock, too. It hurt. I grunted and took a quick step forward to maintain my balance; but I still didn't stop or look around.

I heard Norm laugh, and wondered, my face burning, if anyone had been watching.

"He's really a creep," Mike said. "Did he hurt you, Alex?"

"No," I lied. "But he's going to be sorry. One of these days, very soon, he's going to be sorry."

In a little while, now, we'd have everything we needed to fix Norm, once and for all.

For a moment I wondered uneasily just what the spell would do to him, and then I hardened my heart. Whatever it was, it would be what he deserved.

15

I HAD to pretend to go to bed on Friday night. I took my shower kind of late, after Deidra had spent an hour and ten minutes in the bathroom. Obviously the spell to keep her from monopolizing it had only worked one time. Since I didn't care to risk having the plumbing break down again, I didn't try another spell, though I had considered it.

Mike had already fallen asleep. Dad had been able to twist his glasses around straight so they fit all right, and he'd patted me on the shoulder when Mike told him the story, and said, "Nice going, Alex."

I looked at Mike now. He seemed so small and defenseless lying there in his striped pajamas. We had our differences, but he wasn't bad for a little brother. It made me mad all over again to think about Norm kicking him around.

The magic book was lying on my desk. The spells in it *had* worked, though not quite the way I expected. I walked over and flipped open the cover, and the pages did that slow, lazy turning as if they were in a breeze. Only, of course, there was no breeze in my room.

I put out a hand to stop the pages from turning, feeling that familiar prickle of something I couldn't describe, and looked down at where my fingers held the page.

Jeff had read it aloud before. This time I read it silently to myself, and the prickle along my spine got stronger.

The spells in this book are not to be undertaken lightly by the amateur, for the consequences may be serious. Before invoking the powers conveyed by these pages, the reader should soberly consider the potential results, some of which may be irrevocable.

Was the book warning me against what we planned to do? It almost seemed that way. Yet why else had the book kept sliding off the table at the library sale until I finally bought it? Why did it have my name written in the front of it? Why had we spotted the spell to put an end to a bully's ways, only to have that spell vanish from the pages once I got the book home? It *had* vanished; we'd gone through the book page by page several times without finding that particular spell, and then it had come back, after we'd tried some of the other spells.

Was this one more dangerous than the others, either to us or to Norm?

It had always been other people who were Norm's victims; this time, *he* would be *ours*.

I read the words on the page again, then closed the book. I *had* seriously considered the consequences of a spell to end a bully's ways, and it needed to be done. Not just for our sakes, but maybe for Norm's as well. So far he hadn't seriously injured anyone that I knew of, but if he kept building up his attacks he would hurt somebody, eventually. He'd only bent Mike's glasses out of shape, but he could easily have broken them. He hadn't kept the lid on the garbage can long enough for Mike to suffocate, but he might, the next time. So I had to see to it that there wasn't a next time.

Yes, I thought, it was time to do the spell on Norm. A sensation I couldn't describe came through my fingers from the cover of the old book. Approval, maybe? Anyway, I was convinced the book had decided I was ready. It was time to do it.

It made me feel a bit foolish when I turned away from the book into a normal room with one small light on, and my little brother sleeping under the drawings of animals he'd taped to the wall over his bed. It was so ordinary. Once I stopped touching the book, it was only a book again. Not magic. Not dangerous.

W E had to be there to gather the moss exactly at midnight, so we'd agreed to meet early and get there ahead of time. I even set my watch by the radio to make sure we didn't act too soon or too late and spoil anything.

I'd already gotten a small plastic bag to carry the moss, which I'd scrape off the tombstone with my jackknife. We were each going to carry a flashlight. All I had to do was wait until it was time to leave the house.

I had put on my pajamas just in case my dad came upstairs before he went to bed. He probably wouldn't, as long as we weren't noisy. Across the hall, Deidra was talking on the phone. I couldn't make out any of the words, so I knew she wasn't talking to Shirley. For the past couple of weeks, I'd been pretty sure that some of her conversations were with a boy, and I wondered who was crazy enough to spend all that time talking to my sister.

She'd stop talking altogether if I passed her doorway. Once she said into the phone, "Excuse me, but my snoopy brother is eavesdropping. Get out of here, Alex."

I wasn't deliberately listening. If anything, her conversations with this boy were even sillier than the ones she had with Shirley, so why would I eavesdrop?

I could hear the TV going downstairs, so I knew my folks were still up. If they hadn't gone to bed by the time I needed to leave the house, I'd already decided to climb out the window at the end of the hall onto the roof over the kitchen, and drop down into the backyard from there.

At eleven o'clock, though, just as I was beginning to get really nervous, the TV went off. I crept out of bed and pulled on jeans and a black turtleneck sweater and carried my Nikes in one hand. It was time to go.

There was a strange feeling in my chest, as if it had tape wrapped around it so tight I couldn't get a deep breath. It made a sort of ache there.

I moved silently through the house and out the back door, leaving it unlocked behind me. My fingers felt stiff and cold as I tied my shoes, though it wasn't especially cold out.

Lots of houses still had lights on, and TV screens glowing beyond the windows, so it wasn't scary walking along the street toward Jeff's.

Bucky got there a few minutes after I did. I had scooped up a stone from the driveway to throw at his window when Jeff suddenly materialized from the shrubbery. He sounded excited and confident. "OK, guys, let's go. Look out, Norm, here we come!"

We walked fast, ducking into the Connelly's yard behind some trees when a police cruiser came slowly along the street. There wasn't a curfew in our town, but a cop was bound to stop and check out three juveniles strolling at eleven at night. The cruiser went on past, and we started breathing again, though I still couldn't seem to inhale deeply enough to ease that ache.

When we reached St. Andrew's, the gate to the graveyard was closed. "Maybe it's locked up at night," Bucky said, in a tone that sounded suspiciously hopeful. "Maybe we can't get in."

"It's only a low fence," Jeff pointed out. "We'll climb over it if we have to. No, see, the gate isn't locked, just closed. Come on."

I hadn't noticed during the daytime how many trees there were in the graveyard. I hadn't figured how dark it would be beneath them, either.

Jeff led the way, his flashlight picking out the paths between the headstones. It was colder here under the trees, and a few wisps of fog drifted ahead of us in an eerie way.

"Jeez, creepy," Bucky muttered, and I felt I had to say something positive. I wasn't sure I believed it though.

"It's just a little mist," I told him. "It's no different here than out on the street."

"Yeah, we're used to fog," Jeff said. "There, that's the row that has the most moss. Which tombstone are we going to get it from, Alex?"

Jeff's uncle is a police officer, and he'd given Jeff one of those really good Streamlights like the cops use; the light beam was strong and white and made everything in its path stand out sharply. Behind the headstones the shadows were black and made me feel as if I shouldn't look into them too closely.

"The first one that has moss," I mumbled, and dropped to my knees beside one that was so heavily covered you couldn't even read the name chiseled into it. "This one's OK. Shine the light here, Jeff."

The moss looked almost black, too, and the ground was soggy beneath my knees, though it hadn't rained in three or four days. I got out the plastic bag and my knife, and began scraping the moss off the stone into the bag. The blade made a loud "scritching" against the marble tombstone.

The layer of moss wasn't very thick. I didn't want to get too little, so I scraped over a pretty big area, and had decided we had enough when Bucky suddenly sucked in a startled breath.

"What's the matter?" I demanded, and Jeff swung the flashlight around so it shone on Bucky's face.

"You hear something?" Jeff asked, thumbing the switch so the light went out. We stood listening to each other breathe.

"No, I didn't hear anything," Bucky said. "But it was the name on the tombstone, after Alex cleaned the moss away. Didn't you see it?"

Even before Jeff turned the light back on and illuminated the tombstone, that prickle had returned along my spine.

I stared in disbelief at what my scrapings had revealed.

16

M y hair stood right up off my scalp. It was the way I'd felt when Mike and I watched *The Monster from the Deeps* and this horrible creature had risen out of a swamp and staggered after the screaming heroine.

I felt like screaming a protest too, but I couldn't.

Behind me, Jeff held the flashlight on the tombstone and made a strangled sound. It was Bucky who read aloud the words.

"Norman James Winthrop. Born December 9, 1825. Died October 2, 1885. Rest In Peace."

I finally found my voice. "Norman James Winthrop? Is Norm's middle name James?"

Nobody answered, probably because they didn't know. Jeff reached past my shoulder and touched his fingertips to the final date. "What is it today?"

"October second," I managed. "Hey, this is wild. How come there's a tombstone with Norm's name on it? And today's date—well, I mean today's date a hundred years ago? What's going on?"

"Maybe it's Norm's grandfather. Or great-grandfather, or great-great. A hundred years ago," Bucky said softly.

"But it's Norm we're working a spell against," I choked out. "It's too big a coincidence that we came to get the moss off his own great-great-grandfather's grave! And on the anniversary of the day he died!"

"Maybe that's how it was supposed to be," Jeff whispered dramatically. "Maybe the old man that was buried here can't rest because of what's happening with his great-great-grandson, because Norm is such a crumb. Maybe Norm's ancestor is ashamed and wants us to teach him a lesson and clear the family name."

"Maybe we better just get out of here," I said, folding my knife and sticking it in my pocket. I stood up, sealed the plastic bag with the moss we'd come for, and tucked it away.

None of us said anything after that until we'd made our way along the narrow path between the rest of the tombstones, through the gate and onto the street.

"It must mean something," Bucky said finally, when we were half a block from St. Andrew's churchyard. "What's it mean, do you think?"

"I think that darned book is manipulating me," I said. "Us, I suppose I should say. It practically forced me to buy it, and it tempted us with a spell about ending a bully's ways and then that spell disappeared for a while, and now this. It gives me the creeps."

"Me, too," Bucky agreed, hunching his shoulders inside the light jacket he wore.

Most of the houses were dark now except for a few where people watched late TV. Fog drifted in shreds across the street. It does that a lot in Washington State, at least on the west side of the mountains near Puget Sound, and it had never bothered me before. Tonight it made me walk fast, eager to get home and lock the door behind me.

We passed under a corner streetlight where the fog hung in layers; we could see each other's feet if we looked down right, and we could see each other's faces above the milky streaks, but our middles almost disappeared.

Bucky was excited, scared. Jeff was thoughtful. I didn't know how I looked to them, but I felt a combination of all three. "That book—" I said, then stopped. I wasn't sure I wanted to put what I was thinking into words, even with my best friends.

"Yeah, Alex?" Jeff asked. "What about the book?"

"It suddenly occurred to me. It *has* been manipulating me, you know."

I waited a few seconds, and nobody denied that, which made it even spookier. "Well, I thought it was helping me to do things that needed to be done, but now I don't know. What if the book is . . . evil?"

The word hung in the air like the wisps of fog. I couldn't reach out and catch it in my hand, but it was there. I didn't remember ever using that word before in my life, but it seemed to fit. *Evil.*

Bucky stumbled and went over the curb, then walked backward, facing us. The light still touched his face, which was chalky. The reason I could tell was his freckles. His complexion was usually sort of pink, and the freckles didn't show the way they did now unless he got pale.

"Evil. Do you think so, Alex? What if it wants us to *kill* Norm?"

"Nah," Jeff said immediately, before my heart even completed its flip-flop. "Why would Norm's ancestor want anything bad to happen to him? More likely it's what we said earlier: the old man can't rest because he's got this rotten excuse for a great-grandson, and the book led us to his grave. There's no reason to believe the book is evil, Alex. All the spells we've done have been to make an improvement of some kind: to make your sister stop monopolizing the bathroom, to get people better grades. And all we want for Norm is to stop him from bullying other people. There's nothing evil about that."

"I guess you're right," I said. "Actually, since Jim started getting better marks, he hasn't been quite so obnoxious."

"Too bad Norm already gets good grades most of the time. It hasn't kept him from being obnoxious," Bucky observed. He turned around and walked between us. "And the spell even slopped over onto Don. Neither one of them has been with Norm the last few times he picked on someone, either."

Jeff peered around him at me, though we were between streetlights now and it was pretty dark. "Think about it, Alex. Think of the titles of all those spells in the book. None of them were to hurt anybody. They were all positive things, even the ones we didn't try. I don't remember a single one that suggested maiming or killing anybody. I think you're right that the book wants you to stop Norm. But that's positive. It's not just us that he picks on. It's little kids or anybody he thinks is afraid or defenseless. He needs to learn that the rest of us have feelings, too."

"I wonder why he does it," Bucky said, and this time he was the one sounding thoughtful.

That had never occurred to me before, to wonder why Norm was the way he was. "He's just mean," I said.

"Nobody's born mean," Jeff countered. "I bet he was a cute little kid, like everybody else. What made him turn mean?"

"He lives in the projects," Bucky said. "There're lots of tough kids over there. Well, quite a few, anyway."

The projects is what everybody calls a section of town with low-rent housing.

"You think he's mean because he's kind of poor? There are plenty of kids who are poor who are great. Hardly any of them are like Norm."

"Sure," Jeff said, kicking a pop can someone had dropped into the street. It made a loud rattling sound in the night silence. "Being poor's no excuse. Maybe," he speculated, "he's suffering from low self-esteem." His mother and mine took a psychology course at the junior college, and we'd picked up a few phrases from them. We'd reached his house now, which was as dark as the others in the neighborhood, and we paused. "Maybe the only way Norm can feel important is to push someone else around. He feels like he isn't as good as other people. What do you think?"

"He isn't as good as other people. He's the meanest kid I know," Bucky stated.

Jeff warmed to his theme. "Maybe he does it to get attention. Like, some people get good grades, or are good athletes or musicians. Norm's not especially good at anything."

"I'm not good at anything, either," Bucky pointed out. "But I don't bully littler kids," he said.

I felt as if I should tell him he was good at something, to make him feel better, but I couldn't think what it was.

"Well, whatever his reason is, it's not good enough. We're meeting at Alex's at ten tomorrow to work up the spell now that we have everything for it, OK?" Jeff glanced toward his darkened house. "I better get to bed. See you in the morning."

Bucky needed to go one direction, I needed to go another. He didn't start for home immediately, though, when Jeff had gone inside. "Uh, Alex, how about walking on home with me? I want to talk about this some more, you know? Get it straight in my mind."

I knew immediately that he didn't want to walk home alone. I couldn't blame him too much; I wasn't eager to walk on alone, either, and if I went to Bucky's first, I'd have even farther to go alone. But the look on his face undermined me.

"Sure, OK," I said, and saw his relief.

Nothing happened before I got home, of course. I'd known in my head that it wouldn't. Ours is a quiet town, without much crime, and it's well patrolled by the police to keep it that way. Yet I felt better when I slid inside the back door and locked it.

I'd been kind of nervous at suppertime and I hadn't eaten as much as usual. Now my appetite flooded back, and I turned on the kitchen light and raided the refrigerator.

When I carried my plate upstairs, Mike was sleeping. It seemed safe to have a light there, too, while I ate my ham and cheese sandwich and lime Jell-O.

The magic book sat there, not saying anything to me. I looked at it with suspicion; I wouldn't have been surprised if it had slid onto the bed beside me and opened at the proper page for me to get my next instructions from it, but it didn't do a thing.

That didn't reassure me, however. I knew it was there for a purpose; I was only its agent, to carry out that purpose.

My last thought, before I fell asleep a little later, was to wonder exactly what the spell would do to him.

17

B u c k y brought a Canadian-bacon-and-pineapple pizza with him. The three of us ate it sitting at our kitchen table the next morning while we went over the instructions again, very carefully. We didn't want to mess this spell up and make it do something freaky because we weren't precise.

I had written down the instructions and still carried the piece of paper in my pocket, though I had memorized them and didn't have to consult the paper. For actually doing the spell, we read it directly out of the book, to be absolutely certain we didn't miss anything.

Our ingredients were assembled on the table: the brown rabbit's foot, the toadstool (which was looking a bit wilted, though we'd kept it in the refrigerator), the horse's tooth, and the plastic bag of moss. Bucky was fascinated with the tooth.

"Imagine having an ache that big," he said, poking it with a finger. I thought it was gross and hoped my mom didn't come home and see it lying on our table. She'd probably disinfect the whole place and throw us and the tooth out of the house.

"What are we going to mix this stuff in?" Bucky asked, taking the last slice of pizza.

Jeff and I were still eating; I spoke around a mouthful. "It doesn't have to be mixed together. We just have to assemble it, which we've done. Now we have to read out the exact words, and this one calls for us to use the name of the person to be affected by the spell."

I finished my pizza, wiped my mouth and hands on a paper napkin, and opened the book to the place I'd marked with another napkin. I propped the pages open with a clean table knife and began to recite the foreign sounding words. And at the proper place, I said the name of the bully whose ways were to be changed: Norman Winthrop.

A perceptible tremor went through me then, because I was remembering that name on a tombstone in the graveyard. For a moment I thought that was why I felt so cold, and then I realized that Bucky was hugging his arms close to him, with goose bumps on them, and Jeff had an incredulous expression on his face.

"Wow! What happened?" he asked, and his teeth started to chatter. "It's like we stepped into a freezer!"

There was no smoke or bad smell this time. Only the cold, which was almost paralyzing. The book was still held open with the knife, the ingredients sat in a row on the table alongside the empty pizza carton, and as we watched, a rim of frost appeared on the knife that was lying on the magic book.

Outside the sun was shining. Inside, on the thermometer hanging beside the sink, we saw the red line dropping and dropping. Bucky yelped in discomfort.

"It's going to freeze us to death!"

And then, even more scary, the light that came through the windows dimmed. My chest hurt; it was hard to breathe. It got so dim in the kitchen that it was like twilight.

Had we gone too far? Was the spell going to hurt *us?* I wondered. And then, quite suddenly, the mercury began to rise in the thermometer and stopped at seventy degrees; the twilight went away, leaving sunny patches on the floor again.

The only sign of the cold spell was the goose bumps we were all still rubbing, and the frost that was already melting off the knife, making a wet spot on the pages of the book.

Bucky exhaled a long breath. "Gosh! I thought it was going to *kill us!*"

My voice sounded hollow, and I felt as if I'd run a mile. "It isn't supposed to *kill* anybody."

"It's going to do something," Jeff said. His lips moved as if they were numb. "Something *big.*"

"I wonder what it'll be?" Bucky whispered. "How we going to know when it happens? We don't even know what it'll be."

"Nor how long it'll take," Jeff added. "After what we went through to make something happen, I want to know what it is. What it does to him, and how he reacts."

"It might not happen for days," I pointed out.

"But sometimes the spells work immediately," Jeff said, "like making Bucky fall asleep, instead of the dog. That happened almost as soon as we did the spell."

"If whatever happens is humiliating, or painful,"

Bucky thought aloud, "we may never know about it. Norm isn't going to go around telling what it was."

"Well, I don't see what we can do about that," I said, standing up and putting the empty pizza box in the trash. "All we can do now is wait and see."

"I know what we could do," Bucky said. "We could follow Norm around and watch him."

I stared at him. "Follow him around? What excuse do we give?"

"No excuse," Bucky said glibly. "I mean, the spell is going to cure him of being a bully, right? So we're not in any danger. Besides, there're three of us to one of him."

"If he doesn't have Jim and Don with him," Jeff conceded thoughtfully. "Maybe you have something, Bucky. It might give him the creeps, to be followed and watched, even if he's not afraid of us. Give him an idea what it's like for the rest of us to be stalked."

I still felt kind of wobbly, though the chill was gone. "If the spell doesn't work right away, he could get nasty again before it does," I warned. "It would be great to watch what happens, though, wouldn't it?"

Five minutes later we were on our way toward the projects, where Norm lived.

W E had to ask a couple of little girls playing on the sidewalk which unit Norm lived in. They were all alike, two families to a unit with identical doors and windows and front yards.

"That one," one of the girls said, pointing. "With the rusty bike in the yard."

It also had a window with a crack running across it,

so even if someone moved the bike, we'd know which was the right place. There was no sign of life there, though. In fact it didn't even look as if anyone lived there.

"What do we do now?" I asked. "Go up and knock on the door, tell Norm we're going to watch him until disaster strikes?"

"It's a temptation," Jeff said, grinning. "Wonder what he'd think of that?"

We settled for sitting on the curb across the street. There were so many kids around, playing hopscotch and kick-the-can and marbles, riding bikes and tricycles, skating and jumping rope, that we didn't feel especially conspicuous.

A woman came out of Norm's house and paused on the steps to speak to someone still inside. "I'll be back by late afternoon. If anyone calls, be sure to get the name and number so I can call back."

Norm appeared in the doorway. "You always say the same thing. You think I can't remember?"

The woman didn't answer. He called after her as she came down the walk toward the street. "Why can't I go, too?"

"Because your Aunt Ella doesn't want to see you. It's no wonder, after what you did to her dog. It's a miracle it didn't die after you taped its muzzle like that, so it couldn't eat or drink or hardly even breathe. If that neighbor hadn't found it and cut the tape off, it *would* have died."

"It's a stupid dog." Norm came out onto the cement steps, sounding sullen. "She cares more about dogs than she does about people. She locked me in a closet."

His mother paused and looked back at him. "She

doesn't have any other family, just that dog. And she locked you up because you were rude to her. Now behave while I'm gone."

He raised his voice as she turned away. "I don't want to stay home alone all day. That's all I ever do, stay home alone."

She replied without facing him this time. "If you behaved better, maybe you'd be welcome in someone else's house. Sometimes I can hardly stand you myself."

She walked briskly toward the corner, where there was a bus stop sign.

Once she left, Norm came slowly down the walk to the street. He didn't notice us, but he paused to scrub out the hopscotch game some girls had chalked on the pavement. They were screeching at him as he headed away from the direction his mother had taken.

We got up and set out after him. We had to dodge dozens of little kids and a few teenagers, but Norm wasn't in a hurry, so we didn't have any trouble keeping up.

"Maybe he'll fall in that manhole," Bucky said hopefully as Norm cut across the street.

"It's got sawhorses all around it," Jeff answered. "Why should he fall in?"

He didn't, of course. Twice Norm shouldered people off the sidewalk. Everybody seemed to know him; they stepped off on the grass or into the street to stay away from him. A path angled off through a field at the edge of the projects, and when Norm took it, we did, too.

Some kids were playing workup on a makeshift diamond. A little skinny kid hit the ball and Norm turned and caught it, pegging it to first base. That started an argument about whether that meant the runner was out or not.

"Norm's not even playing!" the batter kept yelling. "So how could he throw me out? I got a single!"

Norm laughed and kept on going. We couldn't see his face, but from the violent way he kicked a discarded can out of his way, we didn't think he was still laughing when he reached the far edge of the field.

He looked around then and saw us.

His mouth went into a flat ugly line. "What do you think you're doing around here?" he demanded.

"Walking," Jeff said. We had come to a stop and didn't get any closer.

"Well, go walk somewhere else," Norm said. He swung around and kept going toward a cluster of warehouses on the next street over.

We followed him.

He reached the fence that surrounded a huge lot where there were a dozen trucks parked. A sign on the fence said KEEP OUT in big red letters. Norm followed the fence until he came to a gate. It appeared to be locked, but he did something to the padlock, and a minute later he opened the gate and walked through. That was when he realized we were still behind him. He started to get red in the face.

"I told you guys to walk somewhere else!"

"It's a free country," I said. "We can walk anywhere we want to." I felt braver, being with a couple of friends, but even if I'd been alone I wasn't quite as scared of him as I had been. I'd kept him from hurting Mike, hadn't I, except for knocking his glasses off?

For a minute I thought he'd take on all three of us, but then he swallowed and jerked away. He picked up a rock from the parking area, which wasn't paved, and hurled it at the nearest truck, leaving a dent in the door.

We stood watching him through the fence. He kept throwing rocks, and managed a few more dents and then a cracked window in the nearest of the buildings.

"Are we making him behave worse because we're watching him?" I wondered uncomfortably. "Or would he be doing this anyway?"

"Let's back off," Jeff suggested. "We can watch him from the baseball diamond."

Norm spent half an hour inside that fence, until all of a sudden we saw him come running from behind a building with a uniformed security guard chasing him.

Was this it? Was he going to get caught and hauled off to juvenile hall? But no. Norm tore out through the small gate, and the guard didn't follow him. Norm came right at us, then stopped a few yards away. His nasty grin was back.

"You nerds don't have anything else to do but stand around watching people?"

"We're only watching *you*, Norm," Jeff told him.

The sun was in his eyes, and Norm squinted a bit. "What for?"

"We're waiting to see what happens to you," Bucky told him. "It's only a matter of time before you get what's coming to you."

Norm laughed. "Says who? You going to give it to me?"

"You believe in magic?" Jeff asked.

Norm was a little less sure of himself now, a bit puzzled. "Why? What's magic got to do with anything?"

I took my cue from Jeff. "Because we put a spell on you. To give you what you deserve. We don't know what it'll do, but we want to know what it is when it does happen. We're waiting to see."

"It'll probably be something to help you understand what it feels like to be bullied," Bucky added. "You know, like if someone bigger and stronger takes your books or your lunch. Or shoves you in a hole you can't climb out of. Or maybe something heavy will fall on you. Like a tree limb, or a part off an airplane."

Norm wasn't amused, but some of his bravado returned. "You're all crazy," he said, and started walking around us.

"Maybe so," I told him, "but that won't stop the spell from working."

He didn't answer. He was moving rapidly around the edge of the ball diamond, not looking back.

"Maybe we shouldn't have told him," I said.

"Nah, let him stew about it. And then," Jeff said, "when it happens, he'll know we had something to do with it. It won't be a lesson unless he knows there was a reason for it, whatever it is."

We followed Norm again, back onto his own street. Several times he looked around and glared at us. We didn't say anything, just kept on following. When he went in his house, we sat down on the opposite curb and waited.

Nothing happened. Several times the curtains twitched so we knew he was checking to see if we were still there. Norm didn't come out, and finally we got hungry and went home. We agreed that we'd come back and watch some more after we'd eaten.

When the spell worked, we wanted to be there to see it. We felt we'd earned that much.

18

W E were making Norm nervous.

He wasn't grinning the way he always had when *he* was stalking somebody. Jeff and Bucky and I spent almost the whole weekend sitting in front of Norm's house, and he knew we were there. We only went home to eat and sleep.

When he went out to play ball with some other kids, we sat on the sidelines and watched him. We didn't boo, or cheer when he got a hit, or when he was called out on third base; we just watched.

On Sunday afternoon the Moores came by. Norm had just been hit from behind by a small boy on a trike, and he was about to pulverize the kid until we all stood up and walked toward the two of them. The kid had spilled into the gutter and was trying to get his tricycle upright, and Norm was hauling off to cuff him when Jeff spoke.

"He didn't even see you, Norm. He was looking at the ground, not at you. It was an accident."

"Little brat," Norm muttered, glaring at us. "Why don't you guys go home where you belong?"

The kid jumped back on the trike and pedaled furiously away as Jim and Don strolled up, licking chocolate ice cream cones.

"What's going on?" Jim asked. He didn't sound hostile, just curious.

"These guys been following me around for two days," Norm said, and for a moment the grin returned. Naturally, since it was now three to three, not three to one. He didn't like it when the odds were against him. "It's about time we taught them a lesson."

"No," I said, "it's the other way around. *You're* going to get *this* lesson." This was no time to ease up the pressure, even if we were now three to three.

"Come on," Norm said, taking a step toward us. "Let's run them out of the projects."

Bucky looked at the Moores in that guileless way he sometimes has. It disarms most teachers, except for Mrs. Lowell. "Hey, you guys been getting good grades lately. You must really be studying."

Jim nodded, biting into the ice cream. "It's getting easier, especially math. Miss Miles went over it and over it every afternoon last week until I understood what I was supposed to be doing."

"And then I got Jim to show me," Don said. "My dad says if I can bring home a C average on my report card, we'll go to every Seahawks home game this fall."

"Great," Bucky said, and he sounded sincere. "I wonder if that would work on my dad."

Norm scowled. "Hey, what's going on? Let's run these guys out of here! Let's chase 'em all the way back to where they belong!"

Jim shifted his feet and took another bite of ice cream. "We're on our way home, Norm. We haven't got time to fool around. Our grandpa's here, and he's taking us to Seattle Center."

"Yeah, we have to go," Don agreed. "See you tomorrow."

They walked off, and Norm didn't look happy with them at all. Not much happier than he was with us.

Jeff had a smile like a cat that's just gotten away with cleaning out the fish tank. "Go on and do whatever you were going to do, Norm. We'll just watch."

Norm said a word most kids wouldn't dare to say in front of an adult and spun around and went off down the street. We fell into step behind him.

We followed him to the shopping center, where he fooled around for a while. He was definitely nervous; he developed a twitch at the corner of his eye.

"The spell's working a little bit, anyway," I said. "He's beginning to know how it feels to be outnumbered or outweighed. Maybe it would be a good idea to cultivate the Moores."

Bucky's face was blank. "What do you mean, cultivate?"

"Like be friendly toward them," Jeff said. He always knew what I was talking about. "You see how they looked when you commented on their grades? They're proud of them. We have to make them feel like they're doing something valuable, worthwhile. If we do, they won't be so likely to want to help Norm punch us out when they catch us apart."

It had already occurred to me that while we were safer together, we might be in greater peril when we were separated. I tried not to think what Norm would do if he got any of us alone, if the spell didn't work. The spell *had* to work, or we'd be in worse trouble than ever.

Norm finally glared at us and headed out of the mall. When he glanced over his shoulder to see if we were still there, he didn't notice the curb.

He stepped off it sort of sideways, and twisted his ankle. I saw the pain sweep across his face, and he said another swear word at us and limped on across the parking lot. A car almost backed into him; he jumped aside and leaned for a minute on a parked Jeep, favoring the ankle he'd just twisted.

"Is this all it's going to be?" Bucky said, disappointed "Just a bunch of little things? I thought the spell would knock his socks off."

"What do you want? For him to be crushed under that car? Or to literally break his neck? All we need is for him to stop picking on everybody," I reminded him. It *was* going to be a letdown, though, unless something more dramatic than this happened soon.

We followed Norm home, and we could tell the ankle really hurt. I guess none of us felt too sorry for him. I know I didn't. I was remembering the thud and the burning pain that followed when he'd hit me between the shoulder blades with that rock, and that raw scraped place on Mike's neck after Norm stuffed him in the garbage can.

On Monday morning we were there waiting to walk him to school. Jim and Don joined him, but nobody said anything, though Norm kept his jaws clenched most of the time, and he still limped slightly.

When we got to school, Jim was the last one of the trio through the doors, and he spoke to me. "What are you trying to do?"

"Make your friend Norm realize he can't be a bully any longer," I said.

Jim licked his lips, still holding the door. George Crane and Bill Solomonson were about to go through the doorway and paused to listen to our exchange of words.

"How you going to do it?" Jim asked.

"We put a spell on him," Bucky volunteered. He does have a big mouth sometimes, but from the expression on Jim's face, maybe this time it was OK. "Now we're watching to see what happens to him. We don't want to miss it, whatever it is."

George and Bill were wide-eyed. Neither one of them had any reason to like Norm; he'd picked on both of them. George's mouth even fell open. "You put a spell on Norm?" he asked.

Maybe we ought to play this for all it was worth, I thought suddenly. Tell *everybody*. If Norm was unnerved by three of us watching him, what could we accomplish with the whole school holding its breath to see what took place?

"It's a spell to stop him being a bully," I said. Beyond the open doorway I could see Norm, where he'd stopped with Don to wait for Jim, and I raised my voice to make sure he heard me. For a moment a surge of power went through me, as if I could really say with certainty that the spell was real, that it would work the way we wanted it to do.

"Wow," Bill said. "I hope it works."

He and George went on inside, walking well out around Norm, eyeing him as if he'd suddenly turned purple.

By the time the first bell rang, I'll bet half the kids in school knew about the spell. By noon, the only people who hadn't heard were the teachers. You could tell by the way the kids kept glancing toward Norm, no matter where he was or what he was doing.

In homeroom and math Miss Miles was gone and Mrs. Lowell was back. So much for our vacation. I still didn't know if our spell had worked on her or not. Though in home room she did seem better. Mom says people get irritable when they don't feel well, and Mrs. Lowell was on medication now, so maybe her disposition had improved even without a spell. I hoped.

"Good morning, class," she said in math. "Please take your seats, girls," she said to a couple of girls who were giggling in a corner.

I decided she did sound less cross than usual. My hopes grew as I slid into my own seat.

"Miss Miles tells me that you all behaved very well in my absence. I appreciate that as much as she did." She picked up her ruler, but for once she didn't smack anything with it. "And I want to thank those of you who sent me cards while I was in the hospital."

I exchanged a startled glance with Jeff. Who on earth had done that?

He shrugged. He couldn't imagine, either.

Kids kept turning around to see if anything was happening with Norm. I could tell he was aware of the scrutiny because his color got high and stayed that way; his ears were positively bright red with anger and embarrassment. Every time I sneaked a glance at him, it was the same.

It helped when Max Thurlow leaned across the aisle and asked me in a loud whisper that Norm surely heard, "What's the spell supposed to do to him, Alex?"

Mrs. Lowell's back was turned as she wrote out an

assignment on the blackboard, so I risked a reply. "Make him stop being a bully, but we don't know exactly how it will do it."

Max nodded approval, and Norm's knuckles got white as he gripped the edge of his desk.

At lunch Jim and Don sat with Norm at the table next to ours. Kids kept whispering and staring, and suddenly Norm pounded a fist on the table and said loudly, "Cut it out, the whole bunch of you!"

Unfortunately, when his fist came down he knocked over his carton of milk. It ran into a lake that soaked his sandwiches and his cupcake and dribbled over the edge of the table onto his lap.

Jim grabbed for napkins, but it was a disaster. And of course everybody kept on watching Norm.

He couldn't eat the mess he had left. They scooped it into a waste basket; Don offered him half a sandwich, and Jim split a banana with him.

"It's working," George said in a loud whisper, a grin spreading over his face.

"I hope this isn't it," Bucky said. "We're entitled to a better show than this, considering what we went through to do the spell."

19

WHEN Norm walked down the hallway, everybody drew away from him as if he had some contagious disease. Everybody but Jim and Don, that is, and then they went into the restroom. We were in the hall between classes, going to P.E., and Jeff and Bucky and I were behind Norm as we'd been for three days now. Bucky was beginning to lament that the spell was a dud.

We were coming up even with the offices, which have windows overlooking the corridor, so they can spy on the kids. The big window from the main office showed us Mr. Hamilton talking to his secretary, and a couple of teachers were waiting to talk to him when he'd finished. Normal. Same as always.

And then everything changed. We all felt it at the same time. A slight tilting of the floor, so Jeff and I lurched into each other. A few kids put out their hands to grab hold of the walls or the lockers beside them. Norm, ahead of us, was in front of those big office windows. But we weren't there yet, and we just stopped where we were.

"Earthquake," Jeff gasped.

We didn't have earthquakes very often, not the way they do in California where my grandparents live. I'd been in one in Eureka that made the chandeliers in their big old Victorian house swing for a full five minutes, and dishes fall off the shelves and break.

I didn't remember ever having one here at home that was hard enough to do any damage; they were over before you even had a chance to get very scared, and then people laughed about them.

This one seemed like slow motion, though I think it really happened very quickly. Because the minute Jeff said "earthquake," that big window into the office sort of bulged—I swear it did—and then it popped out of the frame and toppled out into the hallway. Right on top of Norm.

A few kids screamed or squealed, and then whatever anyone was saying was drowned out by the smashing glass. It splintered into great shards like swords, and tiny pieces of it flew in every direction.

Glass was still sliding across the tile floor when I saw Norm's face. He'd been knocked down, and the broken glass was all around him. I didn't see any blood, and his eyes were open and his mouth, too, so I knew he wasn't killed.

My first thought was we'd overdone the spell. Then the sounds died down, and it was so quiet we could hear the ticking of the old clock on the office wall.

There was a chunk of unbroken glass right on top of Norm's head, and as practically the entire school watched, it slid off and smashed beside him, breaking into a dozen fragments.

Norm stared down at the tiny red specks that appeared on his arms and hands—his only injury as far as I could see—and then he started to scream.

"You did it! You tried to kill me!" he bellowed, scrambling around in all that pile of glass, getting to his feet. He lunged toward me, and I was sure glad when Mr. Hamilton grabbed him by the back of his shirt just before he reached me.

"He did it! He put a spell on me!" Norm yelled. "He could have killed me!"

Mr. Hamilton held him firmly. "It was an earthquake, Winthrop. An earthquake that made the glass fall out. The window's been there a long time, since the school was built, and probably the putty was all dried out and not holding it too firmly. Are you hurt?"

Norm didn't even hear him. "I'll get you for this, Alex! And you, too, Jeff!" He kicked out at Bucky, as well, but Mr. Hamilton dragged him backward fast enough so he missed.

"Winthrop! Norman, calm down," the principal said. "It was an earthquake; nobody was responsible for it."

"They were!" Norman howled, struggling to get loose. "They've been watching me, and following me, and they put a spell on me!"

Mrs. Lowell had come into the hall, stepping carefully around the edges of the smashed glass. "Perhaps he has a concussion," she suggested. "Shall I call for an aide car?"

"Yes," Mr. Hamilton told her. "Please do. You'd better call his parents, too. He's out of his head."

Norm swung around in Mr. Hamilton's grasp and kicked. Mr. Radwicke and Mr. Jaeger came up then, and it took all three of them to wrestle him to a standstill. Even then, Norm's eyes blazed with fury, and he kept yelling.

The kids were fascinated. I was beginning to feel a bit guilty, though I certainly hadn't known what the spell would actually consist of. Norm didn't seem to be really hurt, but he certainly was upset.

The bell rang, but nobody went to class. Nobody even suggested that we should go. We all stood there, listening to Norm scream and cry and kick, until the aide car got there.

"He's out of his head," Mr. Hamilton told the EMT's, who nodded.

"We'll take him to the hospital and have him checked out," one of them said. "Yes, he has a pretty good sized lump on his head. Calm down, kid, you'll be all right."

So they drove away with Norm in the aide car. By this time the kids were looking at *us*.

"How'd you do it?" George asked. "How'd you make a spell?"

"Alex got it in a b—" Bucky began, but Jeff thumped him on the back.

"You heard Norm. He got paranoid when he thought we were performing magic. All we actually did was follow him around and watch him."

"No kidding?" George was clearly disappointed. "I thought it really was a spell."

"You felt the earthquake," I said, taking Jeff's cue. I didn't want to get in trouble over this if I could help it. "You seriously think we could cause an earthquake?"

I didn't know if we had or not. But I didn't want to think we had.

Mr. Hamilton lifted his hands over his head and spoke loudly. "All right, students, return to your classes. Be careful of the glass, now. Walk out around it." He spoke then to Mr. Radwicke. "Thank heaven no one else was hurt. Maybe we'd better keep your P.E. class here to help clean up the mess. You wouldn't have time now for much anyway."

So we got brooms and pushed the glass fragments into a big pile for the janitors to dispose of. I spoke to Jeff under my breath while we were doing it. "I don't know whether Norm learned anything or not. He was so mad it may make him worse than before."

"Maybe not," Jeff grunted, scooting along a huge piece of the glass. "He didn't like everybody looking at him, waiting for retribution to strike."

"Retri— what?" Bucky asked.

"Waiting for him to get what was coming to him. And the best thing is," Jeff lowered his voice, "that nobody can trace a thing to us. Everybody felt the earthquake. Everybody thinks he's gone off his rocker. All the teachers, anyway."

He was right, I supposed. Yet the rest of the afternoon I didn't feel quite as good as I'd expected to feel when Norm finally got his. When the final bell rang, I went to the office where two men were already fitting new glass into place, and asked to speak to the principal.

Mr. Hamilton looked up from some papers on his desk. "Yes, Alex, what is it?"

"I was wondering—" I hesitated, then blurted it out. "Do you know anything about Norm yet? How bad he's hurt?"

He smiled as if in approval that I'd cared enough to come and check on Norm. "Considering the things he kept yelling when they took him away, it's thoughtful of you to ask. I've just spoken to his mother; she called from the hospital. They're going to keep him overnight for observation. He did take quite a blow on the head, thought he doesn't seem to have any other injuries except a few scratches. Very lucky boy, he was. The doctors want to hold him until he gets over this delusion he has that you caused the earthquake." His smile broadened, but I couldn't quite match it.

"He's going to be OK, then?"

"Oh, yes, I think so. They x-rayed and said he didn't have a fractured skull or any other broken bones. When he becomes rational, they'll undoubtedly let him go home."

I thanked him and went out to join Bucky and Jeff in the hall. I told them what Mr. Hamilton had said.

Jeff laughed. "Poor Norm may be there for months."

"What if we've really driven him crazy, though? That wasn't what I had in mind when we did the spell."

Jeff's laughter faded. "I don't think it'll be that bad. Norm isn't totally stupid. Pretty soon he's going to wise up and stop accusing us of causing the earthquake. He'll see nobody's believing him, so no matter what he believes privately, he'll stop talking about it. You'll see, he'll be out of there by tomorrow. And it won't hurt if he thinks we have a supernatural power to use if he gets out of line again."

Norm was still in the hospital though. I kept thinking about him as we walked home. "You know," I said finally, "I think I feel sorry for him."

"I do too, a little bit," Bucky agreed.

"What do you want to do?" Jeff asked. "Go over and apologize? Get him started all over again?"

"Well, maybe it wouldn't hurt to tell him we're sorry he got hurt. He did have a big lump on his head, and some cuts. Maybe if we don't keep pushing him he'll come around. See how much different Don and Jim have been since we did the spell to make Jim get a better grade in math."

"I've got a comic I've read," Bucky said. "Maybe he'd like it to read until they let him go home."

Jeff stopped walking and faced us. "That what you guys want? To go see him and apologize?"

"Not for putting the spell on him," I said defensively. "Just—well, heck, Jeff, we've given him a lot to think about. To know that all the kids in the whole school are glad you got knocked down by a plate glass window can't be fun. And if we make him more resentful, he may go back to being a bully again. I don't think I want to work that spell a second time even if we did save the ingredients for it."

"OK," Jeff said. "Get your comic book, Bucky. And we'll go see him."

We walked over to the hospital, not sure they'd let us in when we got there. They did, though.

We found Norm propped up in bed looking at a TV suspended from the ceiling. He stared at us, pushing the button to turn off the television.

"Hi, Norm," I said.

"How'd you do it?" Norm asked. He didn't sound either hostile or friendly, only neutral.

"Doesn't matter, does it?" Jeff asked. "You're OK. Does it hurt?"

146

"Sure it hurts. What did you expect?"

"Sometimes you have to hurt," I said carefully, "so you know how it feels."

Norm swallowed. "I'd like to know how you did it."

We stood there, not knowing what to say next, until Bucky handed him the comic book.

"Well, we better go," I said lamely after a long silence. "See you around, Norm."

He yelled after us as we reached the door. "I want to know how you guys did it!"

Jeff gave him a sly smile. "It doesn't matter. Just remember we can do it again if we have to."

We took the elevator downstairs and walked out into the sunshine. "What spell are we going to do next?" Bucky wanted to know.

"None," I said. They stopped walking when I did.

"What do you mean, none?" Jeff echoed. "It worked, Alex. He'll think twice before he picks on anybody else."

"Yes." I was convinced of that. "But I'm not going to work any more spells. It's too dangerous."

"Alex! Nobody got hurt, not seriously, anyway!"

"It got too close a couple of times. No, I'm not going to work another spell," I said.

That night Mom said the library was having another used book sale on Saturday and she was putting books in a box to take over there next day.

Mike donated a book on wildlife that he had a duplicate of; both grandmothers had given him the same book for his last birthday. Dad added some of the books he'd picked up at the last book sale.

I went upstairs and opened the cover of the magic

book. I wasn't sure, but I didn't think the spidery old handwriting that spelled out my name was as dark as it had been.

I carried the book downstairs and dropped it into the box.

O n Saturday morning I was at the library when it opened. The librarians smiled at me. As I walked on past them toward the room where the books-to-sell were displayed, I heard one of them say, "I love to see children who appreciate books, don't you?"

I hadn't come to buy, though. Not this time.

Walking between the long tables, I looked for an old blue-black book with the gilt so faded you couldn't read the title of it.

I found it in the midst of some dusty histories and poetry books.

Holding my breath, I opened the cover.

To my relief, my name was gone. I imagined I saw a new name forming, longer than mine, but the ink was so pale I couldn't read it. Not yet.

I found a seat at the end of the room and sat down to wait.

I wanted to know who the next person would be that the book picked out to belong to.

I hoped I'd find out what they did with it.

An old man paused at the table and I tensed, watching him reach out for a book. It wasn't the magic book he chose, though, and I relaxed a little. I'd brought a granola bar, and I unwrapped it surreptitiously; we weren't supposed to eat in the library, not even the part where they held the book sale.

A minute later Norm Winthrop walked it. What

was he doing here? I didn't remember ever seeing him at the library before. Then it dawned on me that for the first time I could remember, I didn't feel a tightening in my stomach when he looked over and saw me. It was very strange when I realized that I wasn't afraid of him anymore. I didn't have the slightest impulse to get up and slip out of the side door before he got close to me.

Eating stimulates my brain cells. At least I guess that's what it was, because all of a sudden I had a lot of ideas.

Maybe I hadn't even needed to use that last big spell, the one that caused the earthquake and made the window break over Norm's head. The day I'd found Norm picking on Mike, it had been the way Grandpa said. What had needed to be done—rescuing Mike before his glasses were broken, or he got hurt—was more important than what was going to happen to *me* if I interfered. I'd stood up to Norm, without any magic, and I'd won.

Oh, sure, he'd hit me in the back with a rock. But that hadn't been as painful as standing there and letting him terrorize Mike would have been. It had made me feel better, to stop Norm. I'd done it once, which ought to mean I could do it again if necessary! Braving a fire was better than letting someone burn to death; facing a bully was better than allowing my little brother to be hurt. And standing up for myself would be better than being afraid of Norm for the rest of my life.

I watched him now, crossing the room, poking around among a bunch of paperbacks with bright covers. I never knew Norm was a reader. I wondered what kind of book he was looking for.

Oh, no!

I almost choked on my last bite of granola bar, because Norm had left the paperbacks and was standing before *the* table, the one where the old blue book sat. He was picking it up, letting the pages flutter apart. I saw his mouth drop open, and then his eyes bulged out.

He glanced around to see if anyone was watching him, and our eyes locked. He looked really peculiar. Probably about the way I'd looked the day I found that special book.

Not Norm, I thought, almost in a panic. It *couldn't* be meant for *him!*

He licked his lips, closed the book, and was turning away when it slid off the table, hitting him on the foot.

Several ladies looked at him, and Norm's face turned red. He picked up the book, replaced it on the table, and hesitated. Then he opened the cover again, and read the flyleaf for the second time.

I didn't have any doubts about what was written there now. No, it couldn't be . . .

And then I started to grin. He saw me, snapped the book shut, picked it up and started toward the door with it. He gave me a scowl as he passed me, but this time it didn't bother me at all.

I knew that book better than Norm did. I knew the crazy things it had made me do, and the crazy way it had made me feel. And even now I wasn't really sure that those spells worked, at least not on other people.

I got up and started toward the door after him.

I couldn't wait to see what that book was going to do to Norm.